Frederick Denison Maurice

Faith and Action

Frederick Denison Maurice

Faith and Action

ISBN/EAN: 9783337105181

Printed in Europe, USA, Canada, Australia, Japan

Cover: Foto ©Andreas Hilbeck / pixelio.de

More available books at **www.hansebooks.com**

FAITH AND ACTION

FROM THE WRITINGS OF F. D. MAURICE

SELECTED BY

M. G. D.

WITH A PREFACE BY

REV. PHILLIPS BROOKS, D. D.

BOSTON
D. LOTHROP AND COMPANY
FRANKLIN AND HAWLEY STREETS

PREFACE.

ONE thing surely is true of Frederick Maurice — that all which he wrote was meant to bring light and help to men. It is not, then, too much to hope that such a collection of extracts from his writings as has here been made by one who is intelligently and deeply interested in them, will find a cordial welcome and a large opportunity of usefulness.

All who have read the very interesting life of Maurice which his son has given us, know how full his days were of controversy. But they know also how far he was from being of a controversial spirit. Now that the controversies have passed away, the spirit of one of the greatest souls in the whole history of English religion may be clearly seen and felt. He who was so brave was very gentle. He who threw himself with such intrepid earnestness into every moral and religious and political question of his day, lived all the time in the profoundest thoughts and truths which belong to all times because they belong to all time and have the Eternity of God. Maurice believed in God with all his soul — not as so many of us believe in Him as an Explanation of the Universe or as the necessary Condition of all thought — but as the very Life of Life — as the Being which was and is and is to come — as the Element in whom we live and move and have our being. Believing thus in God, there could be for him no dislocation of the present from the future or the past. The Eternal was here now. The infinite issues of actions and

iii

lives were already present in the actions and the lives themselves.

Nor could he think of Religion or man's relationship to God as something which might be added to or taken from the life of man — something which a man might win or lose, take up or cast away. It *was* man's life. ⸱To know God and Jesus Christ was to live. Religion, instead of being something occasional, exceptional, the privilege of rare, strange souls, was to him the very flower and sunshine of humanity. It was no harbor into which man fled for refuge. It was the sea on which man's life floated and sailed.

And thinking thus of God, Revelation became to him not the sending and receiving of a message now and then, but the shining of a perpetual sun. All History, all Life was Revelation. An infinite openness of relationship between God and man as between the Father and the Son, finding for itself in the Bible, and in the Christ of the Bible, the supreme utterance of that which all times and lives and books spoke in their small degree, this was what he loved to think and teach.

The days in which we live are a good deal given to contempt of Theology. In this great teacher of our day there was a noble rebuke and protest against that feeble and enfeebling scorn. He was altogether a Theologian. For him all knowledge which deserved the name of knowledge was Theology. Our weak way of talking about Dogma as an excrescence and encumbrance found no tolerance with him. He was no dogmatist, but he got rid of dead dogmas, not by burying them or burning them, but by filling them with life.

Men complain of the obscurity of Maurice. But it is good for us, so complaining, to remember what he himself wrote once to Kingsley — "After all, I care a good deal more that the thing should be understood than that I should be — " And "the thing" — all the great things of which he wrote — have been understood through him by many who have often puzzled over the page to know what their teacher meant. The sources of the Nile may be very dark while its waters are turning deserts into gardens. There has been no great teacher of mankind in whose nature have not met the mystic and the moralist, the seeker after most transcendent truth, and the enforcer of most practical duty. And mystic and moralist never came to more harmonious and perfect meeting than in Maurice.

The result of their meeting is a great spiritual master whom the world has already felt, and whom it is yet to feel much more before his power is exhausted. One of the things which he most loved in life was to feel himself spiritually influential upon men very different from himself; men who, awakened by him, could then do works that lay quite outside of his character and powers. That must be indeed a great delight. It must fill a man with humility and thankfulness. To touch a languid spring, to break the rust off a tight or hindered bolt, to free a doubt with an inspired word, to kindle a long life of energy with one flash of fire, to make a fellow-man see God — there can be no privilege like that. The wisdom which is not able to do that fails of the fullest proof of power and must be at heart dissatisfied with itself. The men who do that are the men whom the world remembers — or, if it forgets their names, it lives by their illumination long after they are dead. High among such men — pure, humble, real, full of insight because full of faith — stands the great spiritual teacher some of whose words are gathered in this little book.   P. B.

FAITH AND ACTION.

I.

LIFE.

HOW easy it is to utter sentiments and to feel their truth deeply, how hard to connect them with real life, to bring them to bear on one's own conduct and on what is passing around us!

**

All our lives through we must learn by teaching; we must gain stores by distributing what we have.

**

Do not let any of us, then, complain that our circumstances are making us evil; let us manfully confess, one and all, that the evil lies in us, not in them.

**

In life and practice words are most real substantial things. They exercise a power which we may deny if we choose, but which we feel even while we are denying it. They go forth spreading good or mischief through society. Surely there must be something solemn and deep in their nature.

1

*_**

The faculty of doing good, by an eternal law, is multiplied and magnified according to the use that is made of it.

*_**

One can find enough that is not good and pleasant in all ; the art is to detect in them the good thing that God has put in each, and means each to show forth.

*_**

The joy of recovery . . . the joy of those who cannot keep their happiness to themselves — who must call upon others to partake of it. Is not *all* joy of this quality? Are not these its characteristics? . . . Try to conceive the most selfish motive for it, still it only becomes joy by bursting the bonds of self.

*_**

. . . All deep truths must be found out, I think, slowly. They lie beneath all experiences of pleasure or pain. We are to grow with them, and in due time they will work upon us and mould us after their own likeness.

*_**

Nothing is good that does not carry us beyond itself.

*_**

When we have some opinion which we are *not* sure of, which we cannot rest in, yet which is dear to us because it is ours, then the impulse to crush those who will not accept it, who cannot see the force of our arguments, is very strong indeed.

**

Only the man who gives, hoping for nothing again, who gives freely without calculation out of the fulness of his heart, can find his love returned to him. . . . We see it every day; and every day, perhaps, we may be disappointed at finding some favors which we thought were well laid out, bringing back no recompense. They were bestowed with the hope of something again.

**

Retirement is good, but not as a luxury.

**

Not the words which are appropriated to the service of art and philosophy, which are withdrawn from daily usage, but those which are passing from hand to hand, those which are the current coin of every realm, those which are continually liable to lose their image and superscription from the friction of society, these are the truly sacred words; in them lies a wealth of meaning which each age has helped to extract, but which will contain something for every fresh digger. The word *I*, with its property of being demanded by a whole community, and yet only capable of denoting a single unit, is a key to that mystery in words which makes them interpreters of the life of individuals, of nations, of ages; the discoveries of that which we have in common, the witnesses of that in each man which he cannot impart, which his fellows may guess at, but which they will never know.

**

What is there in the force of gunpowder that can be measured against this force (*of words*) *?* If we had a barrel of that in our houses, what would it be to these words which we carry with us wherever we go, which we are ready to discharge so freely, with so little recollection whither they may be borne, or what work of death or life they may do?

**

(*A man*) is not dealing honestly with himself when he says there is nothing in him but what is mean and selfish. He may think that he is exhibiting a creditable humility in saying so. It is not humility at all, nor is it in the least creditable. On the contrary, he is often secretly crediting himself with being better than he gives himself out to be, often thinking that he may make a little capital out of his self-depreciation. He will not be humble till he owns that there is a good always present with him, a good which he inwardly desires, a good which he ought to pursue. Then he will begin in very deed to feel the evil which is adverse to the good; he will understand that it ought in some way or other to be cast off.

***

We need not study the records of the past, or the actions of our fellowmen, to learn what the spirit of fear or cowardice is. Each one knows the gripe of it in himself. Each one has trembled before the opinion of Society, or of that little fraction of Society with which he has to do, or of some particular man. Each has, perhaps, known something of that cowardice which springs from self-distrust, from the apprehension of lions in his path, from doubtfulness, which of several paths he should choose, from the foretaste of coming evils. If only some . . . shrink at the thought of certain acts being exposed which they would desire that none should ever know but themselves, is there one of us who has not been made conscious of tempers, habits, states of mind, which he has longed to conceal from the eye of that Judge to Whom he is sure they must be most hateful?

***

The habit of regarding separate possession as the basis of Society, as the end which all Society exists to secure, leads directly to the expressions which we hear so often: "I have paid the fellow for his services; what more can he ask of me?" That is in other words, "Between me and him there is no relation; the only bond between us is that which money has created." That is the feeling on the master's side. And the ser-

vant's of necessity corresponds to it, "I owe him nothing: he has had his work out of me. What more have
I to do with him?" There are men, generous and
noble men who listen indignantly and impatiently to
this kind of discourse, who think it is increasing
(*among us*).

**

You may as well wait for the crowd to pass you in
Cheapside as wait for public opinion to make a scientific discovery, or extinguish a great popular abuse, or
assert a great moral truth; all that work must go on in
closets with tears and prayers, and earnest fightings
against ourselves and against the world.

**

Many of us persuade ourselves, all of us have probably at one time yielded to the opinion that *reputation*
is necessary for the sake of *usefulness*. Every hour, I
think, will show us more and more that the concern
about reputation is the great hinderance to usefulness;
that, if we desire to be useful, we must struggle against
it night and day.

**

It is very good and useful to be reminded that all
mere rules, all that we read of in books, have to do with
flesh-and-blood human beings. Yes, it is good to be reminded of this, even when we have to connect these
human beings with crimes and with punishment. That

surely does not make us feel less that they belong to
our race, that they are of our kindred.   It sets us upon
thinking how many temptations every man and boy-
vagabond is exposed to that we are not exposed to, and
what we might have done if these had been acting
upon us.

* *

States of heavy despondency do not last: perhaps in
speaking of them they depart.   Despondency is hardly
a state of mind: it is the mind's forgetfulness of its
own true state — which is a glorious state, as I need
not tell you.

* *

You are not sent into the world *to get credit for*
freedom of mind, liberality, manliness, sincerity, but, as
far as you are shown how, to bear witness of that which
you know, to testify of that which you have seen.

* *

To own the height and depth, the length and breadth
of the love which is revealing itself in all God's works
and ways, to trace it in a few of its manifestations towards human beings, is better work than to discuss any
opinions.   So best we learn what opinions have meant
to those who have striven about them most earnestly.

* *

Man seeing only himself sinks to the point where
society becomes impossible — where every man becomes

the corruptor and destroyer of every other. Man seeing himself in God, feeling his own relation to God,
grows into the perception of a fellowship and sympathy
between himself and every being of his own race — into
a perception of the loving care and government which
he is to exercise over all creatures of lower races:
grows into this perception, because the divine character
. . . dawns more and more clearly upon him.
And thus the man is prepared for the last and culmi-
nating point in the divine education, that in which he
learns the meaning and ground of self-sacrifice.

***

There is in deed and truth no middle path. The
life of the individual, the life of society, must come at
last to make self-indulgence, self-seeking, self-will, its
foundation, or else Sacrifice.

***

The conscience is not a part of my soul, but is I, myself. Parting with it, I lose not, like Chamisso's hero,
my shadow, but the substance from which my shadow
is cast.

***

The recompense for not distrusting and suspecting a
friend, for assuming that he means you well even when
you cannot understand him, even when his acts would
bear a hard construction, is, that you come to be acquainted with him, to enter into his character, to dis-

cover all the deep hidden sympathies of it. "You
must love him," says the poet, "ere to you he will
seem worthy of your love." It is a paradox in human
friendship and yet every one may have proved it for
himself. We might hesitate to apply the paradox to
our relations with God because they are grounded upon
the principle. "Not that we loved Him, but that He
loved us." And yet it *is* applicable there also. For
He himself awakens in his creature a blind trust, a faith
of expectancy, grounded upon the acknowledgment
that He is that which by degrees He will show Himself
to be. And, therefore, the growth of love and knowledge, and the power of cleaving more strongly because
the attraction is stronger, are always proclaimed in
Scripture as the rewards and prizes of a man who walks
in the way in which God has set him to walk, who
chooses life, and not death.

***

Only three of the disciples were on the Mount.
And only two or three, just at rare times, may feel as
if they were carried into a brighter world, and as if they
beheld things as they are, not hidden by the mists of
our earth. I do not know to whom God grants such
manifestations; but I have no doubt that there are
some, probably those who have some special work or
suffering to go through — humble people, I dare to say,
of whom the world takes no note.

*

The God of grace and mercy gives to each that which he craves for: if we think that all is well with us, He will leave us to try whether all is well. If we find that there is something not well, something that must be set right in us, He will set it right.

*

I dread, for all, *in*difference, not difference from me. . . . We may be of a little use, while we remain here, in giving warnings, derived from the experience of our own blunders, but if we try to compel any merely to walk in our steps, we show distrust, and not faith.

*

We shall profit by all that befalls us. If it is good and necessary for most of us to be humbled — if we cannot be anything or do anything right till we are humbled, then be sure God means all that He sends us for this purpose. Sometimes it may be a great trouble, sometimes it may be a little vexing trouble which overtakes us. One may do the work as well as the other. . . . God knows which will do it best for each of us. Or He may send us good and bright days. They may tend to our humiliation as much as the others. We may wonder what right we have to them; how such people as we should have blessings that we have done so little for.

***

The secret of most of our misery is that we are trying to please ourselves.

***

Do you think it is liberty for a man to be left to do what he likes? I do not know any slavery so hard as that.

***

Distance of time is not always unfavorable to accurate recollection. We often remember a friend's words better, years after they were spoken, than the next day; because we understand them better, because we see how one of them rose out of another.

***

Truth and liberty are inseparable companions, neither can live long apart from the other.

***

The highest life is the life that sacrifices itself.

***

. . . Men say "These things were so different when we were young! How bright they looked once! How they have faded!" We all know that it is the eye which has become dimmer; the things are as they were. Perhaps they never really seemed much brighter; in youth there may have been other shadows, which we have now forgotten. Only the heart is certain that it ought to enjoy, that it is meant to enjoy, and therefore

will persuade itself that it once did enjoy.   It has a
witness in itself that there is another kind of gift from
these, a gift which is directly to the heart, and not to the
heart only through the eye ; a gift that brings the light
by which it is contemplated, and then throws light upon
all things around ; a gift which depends upon no accidents, but which compels accidents to obey it, drawing
strength and nourishment from those things which
seem most contrary to it.   And this gift, which all
men know that they want, is that which Christ bestowed upon his disciples. " *My peace I give unto you.*"

* *

. . . St. John says " HE *hath blinded their eyes
and hardened their hearts.*" We must not dare to
cancel these words, because we may find them difficult.
St. John himself interprets them in the next verse. He
reminds us that Isaiah spake these words when he had
the vision of the King who was sitting upon a throne
and filling the temple with His glory. . . In both
cases it is the goodness, the beauty, the glory, which
blinded the eyes and hardened the hearts. We know
that it is so. Experience tells us that goodness has
this effect upon minds in a certain condition. The bad
that was in them it makes worse. The sight of love
awakens and deepens hatred . . . This blinding destructive effect of goodness and love upon the evil will,
is a fact which we are bound to confess, and to tremble.

***

We never experience either the difficulty of a divine sentence, or the power of it, till we put it in practice.

***

Let us understand that God has been educating us to educate our brethren of the working-class, and all that *we* learn, all *we* are still learning, . . . will acquire a new character, will be valued as it has never been valued before, will be changed from a weight into a power — from the routine of a machine, into the onward movement of a spirit.

***

We may dwell upon bright and hallowed moments of lives that have been darkened by many shadows, polluted by many sins: those moments may be welcomed as revelations to us of that which God intended His creatures to be; we may feel that there has been a loveliness in them which God gave them and which their own evil could not take away. We may think of their loveliness as if it expressed the inner purpose of their existence; the rest may be for us as though it were not.

***

How many of us feel, in looking back upon acts which the world has not condemned, which friends have perhaps applauded, "We had no serious purpose there; we merely did what it was seemly and convenient to do; we were not yielding to God's righteous will; we

were not inspired by His love!" How many of us feel
that our bitterest repentances are to be for this, — that
all things have gone so smoothly with us, because we
did not care to make the world better, or to be better
ourselves! How many of us feel that those who have
committed grave outward transgressions, into which
we have not fallen because the motives to them were
not present with us, or because God's grace kept us
hedged round by influences which resisted them, may
nevertheless, have had hearts which answered more to
God's heart, which entered far more into the grief and
the joy of His Spirit than ours ever did!

**

The worker is, emphatically, *not* a bustler: he cannot be one. To fulfil his character, he must go on
steadily, from step to step: there must be no hurry,
and no intermission. . . . He can, according to
Bacon's grand aphorism, but bring two things together,
or separate them: the rest nature transacts in secret.
The fever of the miscellaneous man, of the man who
hopes to prevail by his multitude of words, is altogether
foreign from him. Just so far as he is a producer, he is
silent and calm.

**

. . Learning has no necessary connexion with
Leisure. But it has the most intimate connexion with
Rest. There cannot be two words which represent

more different thoughts than these two : there cannot
be anything more perilous than the confusion of them
. . . We see a number of men in the Universities,
a number of men in London, with a prodigious weight
of Leisure, but they are certain to be the most restless
people we can encounter.

**

A dull mechanical temper of mind, obedience to mere
custom, impulses communicated from without, not from
a spirit within, a will recognizing no higher law than
the opinion of men, — this is that turning away from
God, that implicit denial of His presence, which makes
it a most needful thing that the call should go forth
from some human lips, and be echoed by unwonted natural calamities, and be received as coming straight from
the mouth of the Lord, "Repent and be converted."
. . . The capacity for manly effort becomes feebler
and feebler. A lion is always in the path to every duty.
It is not the inner life, the Kingdom of Heaven only,
which is forgotten and disbelieved in; the spade and
the plough lie idle; it is supposed that thorns and
thistles are meant to possess the ground, and that man
is not meant to remove them.

**

No doubt every man is to prepare himself, in whatever he undertakes, for the probability of disappointment
and ridicule; that is part of his regular cost and outlay,

which he is most improvident if he does not count be-
forehand and consider whether there is anything to set
off on the other side. But no men have a right to
begin a work which they do not think has a principle
in it that may live and bear fruit after they are dead
and forgotten.

* *

We know not when the final day of decision is to be.
But there is some day of decision in every age, some
great battle of truth and falsehood, of righteousness and
injustice, of love and self-will, in which we must one
and all take part. There is a power of destruction at
work in every society, in every heart. Do not fancy
that you are less in danger from it than your forefathers
were. It is nearest to you when you are least aware
of its approaches, when you are least on your watch
against it. A day may be very near at hand when the
question will be forced upon everyone, and when everyone must give the answer to it " Art thou on the side
of self-willed power, or of righteousness?"

* *

The great problem of all, then, is how to make men
know that they are persons, and therefore that freedom
and order are their necessary and rightful inheritance.
There may be various ways of solving this problem.
One of them may be by teaching household economy:
one of them may be, by teaching what many call an

accomplishment, a refinement. I do not care what influence you bring to bear upon the man, provided it does its work — provided it arouses him to be a man. Common things or uncommon, fine arts or coarse arts, which promote that object, are all precious.

* *

The mistakes of men are not treated by the Divine teacher according to the rule of the great human teacher, that a stick which has an inclination to bend one way, must be bent the other. . . . He admits that eternal life is to be obtained by Sacrifice, and only shows them how the selfishness of their minds is really making Sacrifice, in any true sense of the word, impossible.

* *

. . . In general, people of all ages wish to be roused out of torpor. The stimulus may be of a kind which tends to produce great torpor afterwards; but the demand for it is a practical confession that torpor is wholly unsuitable to our state, that it is quite intolerable. Do not suppose that men, who are working all day for their bread, are in this respect different from their fellow-creatures. The gin palaces may lead at last to stupor and oblivion, but their first temptation is excitement. Every penny theatre promises the same reward; no ease for faculties that have been overstretched, but a temporary awakening to faculties that have been benumbed.

***

We think a man knows himself when he discovers all
the grovelling tendencies which there are in himself,
and reconciles himself to them. Assuredly it is through
the keen sense of evil within them that most men are
educated to wisdom. But that is because the sense of
evil contains implicitly the pledge of a deliverer from
it, because the discovery of a flesh which is not subject
to the law of God, neither can be, is never made except by a spirit which delights in that law, and asks for
help to fulfil it. The understanding heart of Solomon
led him to revere as well as to suspect himself; to revere that in himself which was God's image, to suspect
that which was seeking to make images of its own:
to revere that which united him to his fellow-men, to
suspect and dread that which divided him from them.

***

This age is impatient of distinctions, — of the distinction between Right and Wrong, as well as of that
between Truth and Falsehood. Of all its perils that
seems to me the greatest, that which alone gives us a
right to tremble at any others which may be threaten-
ing it. To watch against this temptation in ourselves,
and in all over whom we have any charge or influence,
is, I believe, our highest duty. In performance of it,
I should always denounce the glorification of private
judgment, as fatal to the belief of Truth, and to the

pursuit of it. We are always *tending* towards the
notion that we may think what we like to think; that
there is no standard to which our thoughts should be
conformed; that they fix their own standard.

**

We do not need a prophet to tell us how very soon
the mere impression of any great calamity passes away
from the majority of a people, when the visible signs of
it are not present. It becomes a topic for men to talk
of. Some may smart under the recollection of homes
devastated, or friends perished; but soon all seems to
have returned to its old course. In many there is a
strange sense of security from the notion that they have
had their fill of startling occurrences, and that any repetition of them can scarcely be looked for in their day.

**

The grand truth that God's forgiveness is the ground
of man's forgiveness, and that God's forgiveness, free,
large, absolute as it is, only reaches a man's heart when
it subdues his unbrotherly heart and makes him forgiv-
ing — a truth of which we are all most imperfectly conscious, and which we are setting at naught continually
by our theories, as much as we forget it in our practice.

**

The more you look into the discussions of different
parties in our time, the more you will find that, however narrow and exclusive they may be, *comprehension*

is their watchword.   We separate from our fellows on
the plea that they are not sufficiently comprehensive ;
we strive to break down fences which other people
have raised, even while we are making a thicker and
more thorny one ourselves.

**

    .   .   .   If we do believe that the Son of Man is Him-
self best able to tell us what the sitting on the throne
of His glory and the gathering before Him of all nations
are, let us listen to His teaching: let us think that
when He utters the words, " *Inasmuch as you did it to
one of the least of these, ye did it to me,*" He proclaimed
that which is the very truth of human existence.

    .   .   .   To us, if we hold fast this truth and try to
live by it, that judgment at the last day will be no idle
fiction ; not a pageant with which we shall dare to trifle,
but a living, eternal verity, which it would be the loss
of all our hopes for ourselves, or for our race, of all our
faith in God to part with.

**

The *talents* might be apparently unequal because the
tasks and temptations of those to whom they were committed were unequal.   But all were adequate, all
might be improved.   .   .   .   They were not absolute
gifts, but gifts to be traded with.   And the difference
between one and another arises primarily from the
neglect of this trading, ultimately from distrust in the

owner. . . . The principle of this parable, then, . . . is deep and universal. . . That with which we are especially concerned here, is the lesson concerning the evenness and righteousness of God's dealings, the assertion that the same joy is intended for all who do not distrust their divine employer, but are ready to work for Him and with Him in His spirit.

*

Be sure of this : till you have done trusting in your own sincerity, you will never be sincere. Till you know how much insincerity is in you, and frankly confess it, . . . you are not in a way to be sincere. But to have a confession set before us which brings this guilt to our minds ; which tells us that it has been the guilt of our forefathers as well as our own ; that, though our circumstances have changed so greatly, our temptations and dangers have not changed,— this is not to make us insincere.

*

. . . I question whether we arrive at the real force of our Lord's words by reducing two actual women (Mary and Martha) into representatives of certain qualities which ought to be united in every character, if it is formed in the image of Him whose inward delight was to do the will of His Father in Heaven and who went about doing good. Martha complains

of her sister, and is rebuked, for her complaining, not
for her diligence. The deeper moral would seem to be,
that restlessness and bustle are not activity, that a still
current of inward life is essential to steady patient
work.

*_**

The high gifts and the low were equally bestowed
by the eternal Spirit. Prudence dwells with wisdom.
A power of dealing with the pettiest details of life is
just as much a divine endowment . . . as the apprehension of spiritual truths.

*_**

. . . Zeal is an excellent thing if it is in a good
cause, and if it does not spend itself in mere love to
those who are present. But there is a zeal which is
not at all excellent. There are those who show a great
deal of zeal in robbing their disciples of that which is
most precious, in order that they *may* depend upon
them and admire *them*.

*_**

To talk to us about judgments, and the preparation
for them, and the sin of being indifferent to them, and
the advantage of owning God's hand in them — how
little of real help lies in all this ! A wise teacher who
knows that we need so much, must know that we need
something more. We need to be put in the way of
humbling our own lofty looks, of laying low our own

haughtiness, of exalting the Lord alone. It is not a
habit which we find specially easy of acquisition, not
one which comes by merely wishing that we had it,
not one which we can afford to practise awhile and then
discontinue. It must be wrought into the tissue of our
lives.

*

" *Whatever you do, do all in the name of Christ,
thanking God and the Father in Him.*" Instead of the
self-exalting life, you have the life of men who are
submitting themselves to a blessed power of good
which is striving to bless them. Instead of the individual life, you have the life of mutual instruction,
edification, encouragement.

*

If Christ is not in every man, Christians can, Christians will, treat all as chattels, or worse than chattels,
who do not bear their name. Very soon they will feel
they have a right to treat men as chattels, or worse
than chattels who *do* bear their name. No faith will
be kept with heretics. . . . No faith will be kept
with those we think ungodly, or who differ from us.
For what have they to do with Christ? . . . Thus
we proceed, in our zeal for Christ, to destroy all the
life and morality which He has brought into the world,
and we are obliged to invent a new morality of our own
to supply that we have lost.

***

In a civilized country — above all, in one which
possesses a free press — there is a certain power,
mysterious and indefinite in its operations, but producing the most obvious and mighty effects, which
we call public opinion. If this can be brought to
bear upon the acts and proceedings of any function-
ary, we suppose that there is as much security for
his good behavior as can possibly be obtained. . .
. If we think with awe of mysterious affinities,
of some mighty principle which binds the elements
of the universe together, why should we not wonder
also at these moral affinities, this more subtle magnet-
ism, which bears witness that every man is connected
by the most intimate bonds with his neighbor, and that
no one can live independently of another? . . .
It may easily be admitted that a reflection of this kind
is suggested when we meditate upon public opinion,—
the insignificance of the agents by which it works, and
the greatness of its results for good or for evil. But
I apprehend no one is able to learn this lesson from
it . . . till he has risen in some measure above it ;
. . . any more than he can estimate the sublimity
of a storm, while he is trembling lest it should in a moment destroy him, and all that are dear to him, or than
he can think of the hallowed associations which a
churchyard at night-time might call up, while he is

dreading lest he should be pursued by some pale spectre.
If we could learn the secret of overcoming this power,
of acting as if we were indeed responsible to some other
and more righteous one; if that conviction could be as
present to us as the thought of judgment which our
fellow-creatures pass upon us; if our whole lives were
moulded by the one belief as much as they are moulded
by the other, we should be able to understand what the
world's judgment can do for us as well as what it cannot do; the very same principle which keeps us from
obeying it would keep us from despising it; . . .
we should have courage to say . . . "Whether it
be right in the sight of God to hearken unto you more
than unto God, judge ye."

Never for a moment let us try to separate, or dream
that we can separate, our individual life from our national. Our vocation is the same in the most private
occupations, and when we are fulfilling what are called
our duties as citizens. Every duty is a civic duty.
We are fighting in our closets for our nation, if we are
fighting truly for ourselves; our soldiers should go out
to open battle against the foes of freedom and order
with the same recollections, with the same sense of self-
devotion as that which we would cultivate at home.
Commonly they shame us; there is more simple surrender, more casting away of themselves, not for fame

or glory, but simply because it is their calling, their
plain duty, than we can pretend to. . . . We
should try to learn from them this indifference to effect
and its consequences; we should try to teach them
what its true basis is, how it is laid deep in God's own
claim that we should be like Him — that we should be
witnesses for Him — that we should do His work.
When once we understand that, self-sacrifice can never
be an ambitious thing. . . . It will be regarded as
the true ground of all action.

***

Sacrifice may be the expression of the two most contrary feelings and states of mind — the most contrary,
and yet lying so close to each other in every man that
only the eye of God can distinguish them, till they distinguish themselves by the acts which they generate.
Sacrifice may import the confession of a child, who
feels that he has nothing and is a mere receiver. It
may import the sense in a man that he has something
to offer which His Maker ought to accept. It may
import the trust of a child depending on One from
whom it believes all good comes, aware that what is not
good is its own. It may import the hope of a man —
an uncertain sullen hope — that he may persuade the
power he supposes is ruling, to give him some benefit,
to avert from him some danger. It may be an act of
simple giving up, or surrender; it may be an act of

barter,— a bargain to relinquish a less good on the chance of obtaining a greater.

*

We know that restlessness has been and is the great curse of ourselves, and of all human creatures. We know that we distrust God through love of visible things — through superstition. . . . And the consequence has always been, must always be, the same. Growing restlessness, willingness to try all methods; new failures leading to new experiments; the impostor who promises help to-day succeeding the impostor who left us more miserable than he found us yesterday — at last an incapacity of understanding how there can be any blessing left for us — is not this what we have felt? . . . Are not the words " They cannot enter into rest," written deep upon the struggles, the confessions even the seeming triumphs of multitudes? But is there nothing better for us than this dark prospect? Is the Love of God baffled by the unbelief of man? . . . Not so.

*

That obedience should be the means of rectifying the disorders of the universe, of bringing back the state of things which self-will has broken and disturbed, of re-establishing the kingdom and righteousness of God, of renewing and subduing the hearts of human beings, this is what we should with wonder and trembling expect; this is what corresponds so blessedly, so perfectly, to the deepest prophecies in the spirit of mankind; this is the very Gospel which has brought light into the midst of our darkness, life into the midst of our death. But we must not change and invert God's order to make it square with our condition; if we do, it will not meet the necessities of that condition. We must not start from the assumption of discord and derangement, however natural to creatures that are conscious of discord and derangement such a course may be; we must begin with harmony and peace, and so understand why they have been broken, how they have prevailed and shall prevail.

* *

We confess that we cannot live without a daily renewal of life. We confess that we cannot separate our life from the life of our kind. Consider earnestly what is involved in that acknowledgment. See whether it does not mean that every faculty of sense, feeling, perception, is awakened in us by an impulse from above; see whether every such faculty does not remind us that we must go out of ourselves if we would be truly ourselves. To be *always* going out of ourselves, *always* in fellowship with the Source of all Good and Truth, *always* communicating what we receive from it to those about us, this is the highest perfection we can dream of; this is the life of Christ; this must be the life of those spirits who have fought the fight, and finished their earthly course. To be receiving nothing, to be communicating nothing, to be altogether shut up in self, this is that Excommunication which we can hardly dream of; this must be the condition of devils.

**

This is Peace,— the peace depending on One who is worthy of our dependence, the peace of not seeking that from outward things which they cannot give, the peace of not seeking that from our own nature which is not in it. The Peace is there, in our hearts, but it is there while the heart is seeking its delight in another, while it is forgetting itself. When it finds its object, it is at peace; it cannot be till then. . . . The world teaches us to claim each thing as our own. It says nothing is ours till we can secure it against other men. We hold this peace by the opposite tenure : we have it only while we care to distribute it, while we seek that every one should share it with us.

**

Far off as this peace may seem to be from us, it is really nigh at hand to every one of us. We must think we pursue it hither and thither, and it seems always in advance of us,— we do not come up with it. But that which we are pursuing is only a shadow; the substance from which it is cast is within. The heart cannot find it abroad; at home the treasure is laid up, though it may be in a chamber we have never visited.

Upon our thoughts of God it will depend, in one time or another, whether we rise higher, or sink lower as societies and as individuals. The civility or intelligence of a people may seem to have grown up, and to be growing, under the influence of a multitude of adventitious circumstances. But, if you search well, you will find that whatever in it is not false, whatever has not the sentence of speedy death written upon it, has had a deeper and more mysterious origin. It has been the fruit of struggles, carried on in solitary chambers by men whom the world has not known, or has despised; struggles which were to decide what power they were meant to obey, and to what power they would yield themselves; struggles to know the name of Him who was wrestling with them.

We find ourselves in a strange medley of circumstances. Some of them we call petty, some grand. Some seem to start out of the present hour; some have on them the stamp and dust of ages. We try to dispose them and manage them. The old legend of St. Peter is repeated in our experience. He asked leave to govern the world for a day. He spent that day in pursuing a single goat over the hills, and had to lament in the evening that it was too wild for his control.

* *

What wild pride and recklessness there is in the sense of health! How miserably are those deceived who fancy that a sick-bed is in itself a cure for natural infirmities, and not an aggravation of them and an excuse for them! What selfishness there is in possession, but oh! how it turns inward, how gnawing it becomes in the hour of deprivation and loss. Various gifts and endowments we speak of as full of danger, and yet the man in the Gospel hid his talent in the earth, because he had only one. The physician, lawyer, divine, may each suspect that the other has some especial means of usefulness, some exemption from evils which he has felt; but the heart knows its own bitterness: not one of them is wrong in saying that his position is full of snares; and that what seem to the on-looker securities, are really dangers.

* *

In the region where there is the greatest awe, there is also the greatest courage; he who trembles most, ventures most; it is on the dry cold level of earth that we walk as if on ice, sliding back as many steps as we advance; now proclaiming some hardy sentiment, taking care the next moment to make it innocent of meaning.

***

Courage is *not* natural to us : it does not come through fortune or the accident of being born in a certain locality, or because we have the blessing of being descended from brave men. A thousand motives tempt us to cowardice in little things; we are afraid to speak the truth just as it is; we are afraid to tell our friends when we know that they are wrong; we are afraid to assert what we know to be right. We court public opinion, private opinion. . . . We require more than ever the help of the old Hebrew seer. We want him to ring in our ears continually " *Thou shalt not be affrighted at them, for the Lord thy God is among you, a mighty God, and a terrible.*" But we shall only hear and understand that voice if we hear also the prayer of the Apostle, and join in it : " *For this cause I bow my knees to the Father of our Lord Jesus Christ, that He will grant you to be strengthened by might with His Spirit in the inner man.*" That Spirit is the true source of the courage, which is gentle, because it is stern and unbending; able to endure all things because it is intolerant of evil; essentially human, because it is essentially divine.

***

It may sound strange to say so, but it is true : those who love the world, those who surrender themselves to it, never understand it, never in the best sense enjoy it; they are too much on the level of it — yes, too much below the level of it, — for they look up to it, they depend upon it, — to be capable of contemplating it, and of appreciating what is most exquisite in it. . . . The sensualist does not know what the delights of sense are ; he is out of temper when he is denied them : he is out of temper when he possesses them: . . . The lover of praise and reputation is continually baulked of the flattery that has become necessary to him. He detects something disagreeable in that which is most highly flavored ; a rough word is a torment to him.

***

There is abundance of goodnatured charity afloat in the world, charity for all sorts of people, all forms of distress. But this is the ornamental part of our existence, the capital or fretwork of the building. The substantial part, the pillars of it, we seem to think are our *rights;* rights to position, property, rank, the homage of others, their gratitude. If these are withheld — the hundred pence which each man has a claim upon from his fellow — with what indignation do we repulse the claims which we had acknowledged that mercy and charity have upon us !

***

We have only fairly to look our evils in the face, concealing none of them from ourselves, excusing none

of them to each other, confessing them all to God. We
have but to understand and remember continually the
utter inefficiency of all physical appliances, if the inner
strength and heart are absent. We have but to claim
our share in all the sins of our country, not thrusting
them upon other men, but owning that they belong to
our evil nature, and how little we have fought against
them. We have but to ask God to take away our pride
and self-conceit, that we may be fit to stand in the evil
day, and having done all, to stand.

* *

It is far easier to feel kindly, to act kindly towards
those with whom we are seldom brought in contact,
whose tempers and prejudices do not rub against ours,
whose interests do not clash with ours, than to keep up
an habitual, steady, self-sacrificing love towards those
whose weaknesses and faults are always forcing themselves upon us, and are stirring up our own. A man
may pass good muster as a philanthropist who makes
but a poor master to his servants, or father to his
children.

* *

The older one grows the more, I think, one understands the worth of that kind of communion which
there is between a mother and her son : how much
other intercourse has grown out of that, and wants
something which belongs to it. But it can never cease.

. . . I am sure of that. . . . The inward influences and illuminations which come to us through those
who have loved us are deeper than any that we can
realize : they penetrate all our life, and assure us that
there must be a Fountain of Life and Love from which
they and we are continually receiving strength to bear
and to hope.

II.

MEN.

. . . THE human agency is a very blessed part of
(*God's*) economy : still, the best anyone of us can do is
to teach his brother how he may do without him, and
yet not cease to care for him.

**
**

Have you found that the man who is in the greatest
hurry to tell you all that he thinks about all possible
things is the friend that is best worth having? Have
you found that the one who talked most about himself
and his own doings is the most worth knowing? . .

. Do not you say sometimes in Shakespeare's
own words, or rather in Falstaff's, "I do see to the bottom of this same Justice Shallow : he has told me all
that he has to tell. There is no reserve in him, nothing
that is worth searching after." On the other hand,
have you not met with some men who very rarely spoke
about their own impressions and thoughts, who seldom
laid down the law, and yet who, you were sure, had a
fund of wisdom within, and who made you partakers of
it by the light which they threw on the earth in which '
they were dwelling, especially by the kindly humorous

pathetic way in which they interested you about your fellow-men, and made you acquainted with them?

**

. . . A wise man does not talk about himself. He makes us honor him and love him, because we feel that that is not the thing he is chiefly occupied about. He does not want to make us worship him: if he could he would draw us away from all false worship of every kind.

**

There are some who would give us only the husks of truths in systems: there are others who would give the price of truths in feelings and sympathies.

**

Christ chose the Apostles from no partial affection, but as witnesses of His Truth and Love to all mankind, and the one who was nearest to Him and received most of His love into his heart was the one whom He called to show forth most fully the love with which He loved the universe in giving Himself for it.

**

The one thought in St. Paul's mind with which all that he says about redemption, forgiveness of transgression and every other subject is connected, is that the blessing of the creature is to have the knowledge of God, and therefore that the great mercy for which we have to thank Him is that He has been revealing

Himself. . . . If the teachers of Christianity would but keep this one thought before themselves and set it before others, what a change it would make in all our notions and feelings and conduct!

* *

Luther reverenced St. Paul, not in the least that he echoed any opinion which Luther had brought to the study of him. It was that he had delivered Luther from a host of opinions, which had been anguish to his soul, showing him that there was a direct access for him to a God of righteousness and truth.

* *

There are comparatively few statements respecting St. John in the Gospels; but everyone which we have, shows that meekness and tenderness were *not* the qualities which he first learned to appreciate in his Lord, and that he was not hindered by any sense of these from desiring to renew the severities of the olden time. . . . Unless the Scripture deceives us altogether, St. John had need of hard inward struggles to become a gentle, gracious, loving man. That soft feminine countenance, — unmarked by a single furrow — which painters have chosen to ascribe to him, can never have been his actually, is not his ideally. The man who would have called *fire* from heaven upon the Samaritans, the man who was sure he could endure Christ's baptism of fire, had no soft features, no sentimental expression. If he was the apostle of love, it was love in a different sense from this. "*Blessed is he that overcometh*" are the words which rang again and again in his ears, when he saw the vision of his glorified Master. He had been taught, through the bitterest inward strife, what such words meant.

* *

Is Israel said to be a holy nation, a peculiar people, a race of kings and priests to God, while yet Israelites are described by such ignominious names, and those names vindicated by such ignominious facts? What is this but the truth which we have been learning from the beginning of the Old Testament? That God created men to be members of a kind, portions of a Society; that as a kind, a Society, He created them to be in His own image: but that the first man, and each man since, has been trying to thwart this purpose, to set himself up as a creature, separate from his kind, separate from God; and that in spite of this inclination, God has gone on continually asserting His original purpose and order, gradually unfolding it to men, and by wonderful processes of education leading them to understand it and submit to it?

* *

How then was Balaam a false prophet? No Jew or Christian says that he was a false prophet because the predictions which he uttered came to nought. . . .

That test of truth, if it were enough, the prophet Balaam could well endure. But it is *not* enough to satisfy the demands of Scripture or of our consciences. A man may be false, though all his words are true, though he has gifts and endowments of the highest order, though those gifts and endowments proceed, as all proceeds, from God, though he refers them to Him and seems to hold them as His vassal.

In whatever form self exaltation comes into the heart of man — in the form of craving for popularity, of intellectual pride, of spiritual pride, in the desire for dominion over others, in the secret triumph of our own superiority — the Balaam sin is working underground. . . . Let our trust be in God and not in ourselves to deliver us from this root of bitterness.

Is it not possible, after all, that a *man* may be more glorious than a hero? that to be on a level with all and to feel that the lowliest is the highest may be better than to vaunt up some great champions and representatives, who make us think even more higly of ourselves than of them?

Johnson said of Burke that, if you met him under a gateway in a shower of rain, you must perceive that he was a remarkable man. I do not think that we can

take up the most insignificant fragment of the most insignificant speech or pamphlet he ever put forth, without arriving at the same conviction.

Mr. Thackeray, the most competent person possible
for such a task, has introduced Addison and Steele
among the *humorists* of England, and has shown very
clearly how the humor of one differed from that of
the other, and how unlike both were to Dean Swift, who
is the best and most perfect specimen of ill-humor —
that is to say, of a man of the keenest intellect and
the most exquisite clearness of expression, who is utterly
out of sorts with the world and with himself. Addison
is on good terms with both. . . . He does not
go very far down into the hearts of people : he never
discovers any of the deeper necessities which there are
in human beings. But everything that is upon the
surface of their lives, and all the little cross currents
which disturb them, no one sees so accurately, or describes so gracefully.

Goethe seems to me the most perfect specimen of a
genus of which I do not desire to see the multiplication,
but which in itself is very valuable. The age of mere
self-culture is over, but we must not lose the lessons it
taught.

I can never forget one sentence of Mr. Buckle, which I confess I prize above all his statistics and all his theories on civilization. He said that no mere arguments for Immortality had ever had much weight with him, but that, when he remembered his mother, he could not disbelieve in it. Such a testimony from a man who so greatly exalted the Intellect, who in words, at least, treated Morality as poor in comparison with it, seems to me of unspeakable worth.

Men's unfaithfulness in little things corresponds to their unfaithfulness in great.

The temptation of Savonarola and of every man possessing remarkable endowments and feeling certain of the purpose to which he should devote them, is to think of himself as under some economy different from that of other men. Though in his moments of highest inspiration he claims them all as fellow heirs with him, — though the very secret of his power lies in his sympathy, yet he is continually apt to fancy (and how fearfully does the adoration of crowds increase and perpetuate the delusion!) that he is an altogether different being from those who hang upon his lips. Hence come the pretensions, and sometimes the dishonorable efforts to support them, which have defiled the lives of men essentially brave and true, and have caused them their greatest sorrows and humiliations.

**
* **

It does not signify one jot whether God satisfies our notion of what an inspired man ought to be. It does not signify a jot whether we have a notion on that sub-ject or not, further than this, that if it interferes with our learning what is good for us to learn — and recog-nizing truth where we meet with it, and being true ourselves — the sooner we part with it the better. De-pend upon it, the inspiration of these men was not something which was imparted to them that . . . they might be more separate from us. It was given to them to bind them more closely to those among whom they dwelt. . . . It was given to them that they might be helpers to all men in all times to come, who must be taught of God, yes, and be inspired by God, if they are to do any true act or utter any true word. It was given them that they might teach men in all ages to come, not to think themselves safe because they have a calling from God and gifts from God, but to under-stand that the greatest perils attach themselves to that honor, that they are only safe in holding it when they refer it all to God, and use it wholly for their brethren.

**
* **

Just as St. Paul and the Galatians had this flesh and this Spirit fighting in them, so have you and I. Just as the flesh was drawing them down to low vile things, to those things that ruin the body and soul and set us at war with each other, so it is with you and me. We are not different, so far, from other men. Christians have not a whit better natures than Jews or heathen . . . oftentimes Jews and heathen do good things which should make us ashamed.

* * *

You cannot help reverencing the man who gives himself for his family, his country, his conviction. You cannot help despising the man who gives up his family, his country, his convictions, to save himself. You are sure the one attains the blessings which he seems to abandon, that the other abandons the blessings which he seems to attain. Alas, alas! it has been supposed that, in our religious life the doctrine is reversed. There, it is said, we are to be self-seekers.

* * *

I find it a good rule when I am contemplating a person from whom I want to learn, always to look out for his strength, being confident that the weakness will discover itself, so far as it is good for me to be aware of it, without seeking for it.

* * *

An unknown monk, whose very name is disputed, though he is called Thomas á Kempis, writing in uncouth Latin and expressing more than an indifference for the scholasticism of his time, has had an influence deeper and more widely-spread than that of the most learned men, only because he spoke of an unseen Teacher who conversed with the consciences of men and to whom they might turn in their troubles and their ignorance. The lessons of this monk did not cease to be recognized when another monk of firmer and clearer purpose (*Martin Luther*) spoke to the Consciences of his contemporaries of One who could deliver them from the burthens which doctors and Systematisers had laid upon them.

***

Let none say — that in Jacob's case or any other — the sin consists in pursuing a glorious and righteous end by unrighteous means. If the true end were clearly before the inward eye, the way to it would be clear also. It is because our eye is not single; because there are perplexed, contradictory images floating before it — Self mixing with God — . . . that we prefer an irregular and tangled course to a straight one. If the disciples of Loyola had fully settled in their minds what end God had set before them as the prize of their high calling, there would have been no crooked acts in their policy.

***

The Apostles thought that they could suffer for Christ because they loved Him. They were right in

believing that love is the ground of all action and of all
suffering, but they were utterly wrong in supposing
that their own love could be the ground of either.   If
this love were in any degree an effort of their own, if
it were not God's love working in them, it would prove,
as He had warned Peter that it would, the weakest of
all things.

Christ calls them no longer servants, but friends, because servants only know what they are to do, without
knowing why they are to do it; whereas He has told
them the very secret of His Father's mind.   .   .   .
It is not that the friend is less under authority than the
servant.   It is not that the one does what he is bidden,
and the other may do what he likes.   It is that the
friend enters into the very nature of the command —
that it is a command which is addressed to his will,
and which moulds his will to its own likeness.

Years of hard adversity and suffering do not of themselves fit a man to reign; they may be worse than
wasted upon him: he may come out of them more reck-
less and heartless, more ignorant of any government
exercised over himself, less conscious of any responsibility for the government which he exercises over
others, than he went into them.   For our own individual benefit, as well as for the sake of nations we should

lay this doctrine, hard though it be, to heart. Adversity is, in itself, as little gracious as prosperity. Moral death may be the fruit of one as much as of the other. It was otherwise with David, not because adversity had any especial influence over him, which it has not over us, but because he accepted it as God's punishment and medicine, because he believed that God would do the good for him which adversity could not do.

It has been the belief of all earnest men of all schools that the sop given to Judas was a last love-token, and that the entrance of Satan into him after it had been received, expresses that last defiance of love, that utter abandonment to the spirit of selfishness, which precedes the commission of the greatest conceivable crime.

The kingly lesson and the human lesson are nowhere more intimately united than *in the life of David.* That which enabled David, crushed and broken, to be more than ever the man after God's own heart, to see more than ever into the depths of wisdom and love in that heart, was also that which fitted him to be a ruler, by understanding the only condition on which it is possible for a man to exercise real dominion over others, viz., when he gives up himself, that they may know God, and not him, to be their sovereign.

***

It is in the quiet times that a man is tested. Then we find out not only what he can do, but what he is; whether his zeal for righteousness means that he will obey it: whether his hatred for what is false implies an adherence to the true.

***

There are moments . . . in the mind of the dullest, most prosaic man when unknown springs seem to be opened in him, when either some new and powerful affection, or quite as often the sense of a vocation, fills him with thoughts and causes him to utter words which are quite alien from his ordinary habits and yet which you are sure he cannot have been taught by any other person — they have in them such a pledge and savor of originality. You say, involuntarily, "He seemed for the moment quite inspired, he became another man." Are you not also half inclined to say, "Now for the first time the man has come forth? Hitherto a cold barren nature or a formal education, has choked up the life that was in him : now it is bursting through artificial dams, through mud barriers. Now we can see what is in him."

***

I agree with Carlyle that Cromwell on the whole understood his time better than all who lived in it: that he discovered the godly idea which was underneath the reverence for laws and charters in the **Parliament**, and that which was underneath the monarchical idolatry in the Cavaliers : that he swept away the pedantries of both and brought out the truth of God's government in its nakedness. This is honor enough for any man, and all praise to Carlyle for assigning it to its rightful owner.

***

I am glad you have seen Gladstone and have been able to judge a little of what his face indicates. It is a very expressive one : hard worked, as you say, and not perhaps specially happy; more indicative of struggle than of victory, though not without promise of that. I admire him for his patient attention to details, and for the pains which he takes to secure himself from being absorbed in them by entering into large and generous studies.

***

Bacon reverenced the study of Nature more than he did the study of Man ; and no wonder! For he found out what a beautiful order there was in Nature ; and, though I believe he looked for an order in human affairs too, and sometimes discerned and always wished for it, yet there is no denying that he had a keen eye for the disorders and wrong-doings of his fellow-men, and that he rather reconciled himself to them than sought to remedy them.

**

We owe Jeremy Taylor, the Prince of Royalists and Episcopalians, Milton, the grandest of the Puritans and Republicans, to the faith which the Civil Wars enkindled in both, to the sufferings which both endured. And the man who was better known to the people of England than either of these, the man who has expressed the deepest anguish and the highest hopes, John Bunyan, owes the power which he has exercised, first, no doubt, to the reality of his own inward struggles, but much, also, to the prison at Bedford in which he dreamed his true dream.

**

The age of Elizabeth is the glorious age of our literature only because it is the great working age of the nation; one in which all thought was connected with actual business, and was used for the interpretation of it. In action our writers on Government and Polity were formed. You would expect to find Hooker, perhaps, cultivating his faculties and acquiring his calm wisdom in some monarchical retreat. You find him rocking his child's cradle, shearing sheep, listening to the objugations of a very troublesome helpmate. Our noble Spenser will at least dwell chiefly in a fantastic world. On the contrary, his fairyland is his common native land. . . . His supposed allegory mixes with all common daily transactions. It was in that battle

for life and death in which every one of us is engaged
that his Sir Guyons and Artegalls and Britomarts and
Arthurs proved their swords and won their laurels.

**

A few years ago it might have been thought that
Shakespeare ought to have no place in a Lecture on
Learning. We should have been told that he was the
great type instance of the force of original genius without learning. I do not anticipate any such objection
now. I think all are agreed that historical learning,
biographical learning, humane learning, in the largest
sense of the word, belonged to him, and that it did not
drop upon him from the clouds ; that he acquired it ;
that his genius enabled him to win it and use it, but
was not in the least a substitute for it. Most assuredly
he did not obtain it in leisure, or in any school that ex-
empted him from intercourse with the coarsest persons
and occupations. If he had merely read the old chronicles of England, he might have commented on them,
much as others have commented on him. But he used
them to interpret the actual world in which he lived,
and so both pages became illuminated.

**

When I speak of Robert Burns, it is not with the in-
tention of descanting on his powers, far less of demand-
ing any new wonder for them. How good it would
have been for him and his contemporaries if they had

wondered less, if it had seemed to them nothing at all surprising that an Ayrshire peasant should think more freely and speak more nobly than those who had been trained amidst the forms of artificial life, who were in less close intercourse with that which is native and homely! For then they would have sought less to remove him out of his sphere into theirs; they would have wished more to profit by his strength, than that he should be a sharer in their weakness.

*_**

Take away from a man all the injurious influence that it is possible to take away; not because circumstances are his rightful masters, but because these influences lead him to think that they are, and to act as if they were. Take them away that he may know what has robbed him of his freedom, whose yoke needs to be broken if he is not always to be a slave. And since the man soon discovers, — since his worship of circumstances is itself an acknowledgment of the discovery — that the tyranny which is over him is a tyranny over his whole race, we shall never give him any clearness of mind or any hope unless we can tell him that the Spirit of Selfishness is the common enemy, and that he has been overcome.

*_**

A man may feel that he is called to a work long before the moment arrives when he can perform it, long

before the outward event occurs, which corresponds to
the inward impulse and explains its full meaning.
Such intervals, no doubt, make great demands upon the
faith and patience of him who is appointed to pass
through them. There is the strongest temptation to
doubt whether that which seemed to give a law and
purpose to his life was not itself a dream. There is a
temptation to create the occasion for speaking or acting
before it arises. But the delay is an education which
is profitable in proportion as the original inspiration
and conviction are kept alive.

*

Micah does not make the falsehood of the prophet
consist in this, that he *pretended* to be taught when he
had no Divine Teacher, but that he abused the divine
teaching to vile mercenary ends, that, being conscious
of a spiritual power and illumination, he acted as if his
words were his own, and he might sell them to the service of a great man or a mob. The sacredness of words
almost overwhelms the mind of the prophet; he knows
them to be powers greater than all which the mightiest
animals can put forth, greater than the most wonderful
energies of nature. And these, even these, the false
prophet thinks he may play with, not considering that
he is poisoning the very source of a nation's life, that
he is leading men to believe in a Spirit of lies, instead
of a God of truth.

***

Everything is received according to the character and capacity of the receiver. How should a set of quarrelsome and factious men know anything about the unity of God?

***

The man of profoundest science is, and must be, a little child; he must cease to see himself reflected in the things about him, he must be content to see everything as it is revealed by its own light, not as it is measured and colored by his light. Of such, then, must be the Kingdom of Heaven: only those who can take everything as a gift, who think of the object, not of their own sight or faith, of Him who works in them, not of their own acts, can be the real brethern and fellow-citizens of Him who glorified not Himself, but His Father who sent Him.

***

Every man has the capacity of righteousness, the capacity of evil. Let him be ever so righteous, he must become evil the moment he ceases to trust in God and begins to trust in himself. Let him be ever so evil, he must become righteous the moment he begins to trust in God and ceases to trust in himself.

***

"Give up the thing which thou lovest better than God, and thou wilt know what He is; thou wilt have treasure in heaven." Here was the test. He had never known before what his heaven was: now he found it out. The life he was seeking was the earthly life, though he called it eternal life. . . . It is not the Evangelist's business to give us the issue of the story. One cheering hint they do give us, upon which we may build plausible conclusions respecting the history of the young man. He went away sad. He had learnt to know himself as he had never known himself before, to have a discontent with himself which he had till then never experienced. All good may have come out of that sadness.

**

As some evil tendency or temper, which exists in a man forces itself on his notice, or is forced upon him by the criticisms and admonitions of others, he refers it to some of the circumstances by which he is hemmed in. Has he not a right to do so? Can he not prove his case? That effeminate slothful disposition — cannot he explain to himself clearly what early indulgence, what ill-health, what inherited morbidness begot it in him? . . . That loss of truth in words and deeds, cannot he trace it up to frauds practiced on him in the nursery? . . . But for riches, would he have been so hard and indifferent to others? But for poverty and successive disappointments, would he have been so sour and envious? In this way we reason about our-

selves; we deliberately assign an origin to the evil
within us; can we refuse the advantage of the same
plea to our fellows? Do we not blush when we tell
any man, "You ought to have been so different."
Have not a thousand influences that we know acted
upon him for evil, which have not acted upon us?
May there not have been tens of thousands which we
do not know?

**

There is no case in all our Lord's discourses, in which
the recompense which he proposes to man, does not
consist mainly in the deliverance from the selfishness
which is his great torment and oppression, but upon
which, alas, the followers and ministers of Christ have
been content to build their notion of His kingdom in
this world and the world to come.

**

Was the steward wrong in thinking that he was
meant to win the love of these people about him? or
that the treasures which God had given him were to
be the means of winning it? No, surely, he was right;
he made the discovery in a roundabout way, which,
if he had made it before, would have changed him
from an unfaithful into a faithful servant. . . .
Use the money which God gives you for Him, not for
yourselves, and it will bring in friends who will not
merely give you the temporary refuge which the cast-

off servant sought, but will receive you in your hours
of weakness and sorrow into their very heart of hearts,
will bear you with them when they are kneeling in the
presence of their Father.

Noah was verily certain that there was an end de-
signed for the wickedness of men. When it would
come he might not know; but it would come. . . .
Such faith, once cherished, is fed day by day; it grows
stronger through the very sight of the evils which are
so appalling; it becomes deeper as they become deeper.
. . . The man who holds it, acts upon it. . . .
There is called forth in him, through his faith, the
foresight and wisdom, which are every day departing
from the heartless anxious self-seekers, who are in continual dread of danger, and are continually hunting
after safety and comfort. But there is called forth in
him also, by this same faith, an earnest interest in his
fellow-men.

A man who has been what is called lucky or fortunate in all his enterprises, may feel as if he had no one
to thank but himself for what he possesses, or, if anything but himself, some power which does not especially want his thanks, and will not set any store by
them. A man who has failed in whatever he has un-

dertaken, may look upon earth and heaven as if they
were conspiring against him. But a man who has
waited long for some good, which has seemed to him
more blessed each day that has *not* brought it to him,
and yet has also seemed each day more improbable —
who has been sure from the first, that, if it ever came,
it must be a gift from one who watched over him and
cared for him, and who, for that very reason, has gone
on trusting that he shall receive it . . . — such a
man, when the dream of his heart becomes a substantial reality, has a sense of grateful joy, which turns to
pain, which is actually oppressive, till it can find some
outlet. . . . Out of such feelings comes the craving for the power to make some sacrifice, to find a
sacrifice which shall be not nominal, but real.

* ***

How can a man who has reposed in the justice and
affection of a fellow-man, entertain a suspicion that he
is requiring something of him which is inconsistent
with both, and merely let that suspicion dwell as one
of the citizens of his heart? Will it not cause a revolt among all the rest? He can have no peace till he
sees through his doubt, till it is cleared entirely away.
And if he has perfectly trusted in his friend, if he is
one to whom he has always bowed in submission, who
has taught him all that he knows of what is right and
true, he will say, " I do not understand this suggestion

of yours. If you mean by it what I mean, all is over
with me — my faith is gone. But that cannot be. I
will leave nothing undone that will help me to find out
what it is you really wish of me: at all events, I give
myself into your hands." Conceive such a trust as
never can be put in the righteousness of any human
creature, and this is Abraham's story.

* *

If a wise teacher, or tender wife or sister, may change
the whole tone and character of a man's feelings towards one who has grieved him, not by insisting upon
his hiding them, not by refusing to sympathize with
them, but by the very gentleness which expresses itself
in that sympathy; do you think that a Divine Being
will not have some more effect upon the mind of a
worshipper in transfiguring his whole mind, in drawing
out the truth which is hidden under his complaints, in
severing them from their earthly ingredients? I could
not understand worship to mean anything, if I did not
believe this. I should look upon it as a mere phantasy
and delusion. As I look upon it to be the greatest of
all realities, I hold that in it, and in it alone, one is
taught what a difference prayer wrought in David's
mind — how much David's actions were affected by
David's praying, and yet how little we must measure
the sense and spirit of his prayers by the inconsistency
of his acts.

**
*　**

Instead of instructing us that the habit of mind
which leads us to climb the hill of the Lord, and the
habit of cherishing high thoughts of ourselves, are of
the same kind, (David) assumes that one must destroy
the other; he who aspires to that height must think
meanly of himself. . . . Did you ever meet a man
without any lofty aspirations who was lowly in his
own eyes? What is there to make him so? He measures himself by the standard of people around him.
If any rise above his own level, he can discover some
flaw in them which restores his self-complacency; "he
does all that he thinks it necessary to do; he is all
that he wants to be." This is not what we commonly
understand by humility.

**
*　**

I do not find that I feel less bitterly (towards men)
by saying that I ought to be charitable, and pretending to myself that I am, or by adopting large and
general phrases concerning humanity, or by telling
myself that of course such or such an unkind word or
unkind act does not really move me. No man who
knows himself will trust to these tricks. . . . Nor
is it possible, nor is it right that we should be without
objects of hatred. We cannot be so but by the ex-
tinction of some of our deepest and strongest feelings;
nay, but by ceasing to love. What we want is to hate

the evil in ourselves and in all those who hate us; so we learn really to love ourselves, and to love others as ourselves.

A judge who makes laws, instead of administering them, is not so dangerous a man as a priest who undertakes on his individual responsibility, or merely in general dependence upon the guidance of God's Spirit, to frame devotions for a number of people who happen to acknowledge him as their spiritual director. . . . More and more they will become utterances of personal feelings, less and less they will assume God's teaching as the real spring of these feelings — less and less though there be a repeated reference in words to the divine Spirit. . . . For there is surely no deeper error, no greater denial, than that which is implied in the notion that a sudden, momentary burst of passion comes from the divine afflatus, and that He who is emphatically the Spirit of Order, of Peace, of continuous Life, is not the author of those acts which are preceded by deliberation and reflection. A true Church . . . ought, I conceive, to provide us some common education, which may be useful in preparing our minds both for sudden emergencies and for steady exercises. Prayer has to do with the one as much as the other.

*_**

When the Apostle (Paul) says, "Work out *your*
own salvation, it is God that worketh in *you*," he surely
means us to understand that the work which each is
carrying on is not a solitary one, that numbers are
affected by it besides himself, that all true workmen
are taking part in it. The temptations of men are
various in their outward forms; this evil tendency is
more predominant in one man than in another; but
the slavery into which they bring us is the same, and
the salvation from it must be the same. The slavery
is the dominion of self; the man who is overcome by
lust, by vanity, by anger, alike separates himself from
his kind, and becomes shut up in himself. Therefore
the Scripture is wont to describe all evil under the
name of "covetousness," the desire of things for our
own sakes, whatever those things may be. . . . A
Church lives only so far as she resists this covetousness—so far as she encourages her members to feel
that they are striving together for a common object,
which God wills that all should possess together; so
far as she teaches them that He is working with us to
save us from the selfishness which makes the pursuit of
this common object and the attainment of it impossible.

*_**

Supposing that you could ever say of the life of a
man, "This life perfectly expresses the mind and pur-

pose of God, this life perfectly shows the life that is in Him "—then you would say, "This is the Word of God. In Him God speaks out Himself. In him God manifests Himself." You would not mean merely that something which he spoke proceeded from God, and declared what He intended or willed. You would mean that he, the whole person, was and is the Word of God.

* *
*

A man thinks about himself, dwells in himself; the rest of the universe lies in shadow. It is not that he has not continual transactions with other people; it is not that they do not supply him with things that he wants: it is not that he could dispense with them. But all they do is only contemplated in reference to him: they work and suffer and think for him. It is not that the things which he looks at are indifferent to him; he depends upon them: whether he has less or more of them is his chief concern. But he does not wonder at them or enjoy them; they, too, are only his ministers. Emphatically, then, he has no fellowship with men, no fellowship with Nature.

* *
*

. . . (God) would not be seeking the good of His voluntary creatures, if He did not raise them above themselves; if He did not give them a perfect, absolute object to behold and to dwell in. Those of our age who speak so much about the glory of humanity, affirm that man wants no such object, or cannot attain it if he does. Either it is really the satisfaction of all his wants, or else the only one he can hope for, to be a Narcissus, ever beholding his own beauty, and becoming more and more enamoured of it. I am aware that many who use this kind of language, would protest strongly against the notion that man becomes necessarily a *self*-worshipper, a seeker of his own glory, because he seeks the glory of his race or kind. I admit the distinction; it is a very important one. What I desire earnestly is, that they would ask themselves how it may be practically realized. Humanity cannot be contemplated merely as an abstraction; it must be seen in some one. For a time we may choose a favorite hero, and think that he embodies all we covet to behold. Imperfections appear in him, or he does not meet the new cravings of our mind; he is discarded, another is raised up, who has a shorter reign. We discover that we must not exalt one against another; each one carries in him the nature of all; each man has that nature very near to him. A great and wonderful conviction! but if existing alone, sure to turn into that state of mind which I just now spoke of. Around, beneath, above, the man finds no object so worthy of his delight, admiration, adoration, as himself. . . . I believe we are all haunted by this tendency

to self-glorification every day and hour of our lives.
. . . It signifies not under what pretext, philosophical, political, theological, we build altars to ourselves; the worship is, in all cases, equally accursed.
To throw down these altars . . . this must be our
work. But, if we have commenced this process, where
it always should commence, in our own hearts, we
shall know that we can only drive out the false by
turning to the true.

*
**

An individual Christian is often very furious and
intolerant at a certain stage of his life. For the conviction that he exists to proclaim a truth which con-
cerns all men, and which it is miserable for men to
reject, mingles strangely and incoherently with the
thought that this truth is *his* opinion which *he* is to
defend against all assailants, which *he* is to establish.
Hence a fierce effervescence, like that produced by the
meeting of an acid and an alkali; hence, oftentimes,
indifference when that effervescence has subsided, like
the neutral salt in the other case. And, if the result
be otherwise, it is always, I believe, because God substitutes the certainty which comes from dependence
on Him for the positiveness which is the result of confidence in ourselves or in any human authority.

***

Who will guard the guardians? who will teach us to honor that which in itself is weak, while we are strong? This was the problem which all earnest citizens and statesmen had to work out. If they thought they could solve it by their sage maxims and skilful contrivances, the passions in the hearts, the strength in the arms of those whom they ruled, defied and mocked them. The helmsman who depended upon his tricks and contrivances for keeping the sea in order, had to find that there is another law governing it which he must learn, to which he must submit, which he cannot alter. The manliness and wisdom of the Roman consisted chiefly in that he understood this truth better than most men; he trusted less to his sagacity and more to facts; he perceived that he could only govern by consenting to be governed.

***

When you consider how after eighteen centuries, Passion Week is still remembered in every city in Europe — you try to imagine what those must have felt who were on the spot just at the moment, and who had all personal attachment and reverence to deepen their amazement. Perhaps they will not be able to speak at all; if they do, what words will come from their lips! All such expectations are disappointed. These men are like other men. They are

perplexed and bewildered. They take no measure of
the events which they have witnessed. The events
must mean something: what that something is, they
desire to know. There is a gloom over their hearts;
a misty sorrow; the sense of a blank; a craving for
some interpreter of their own strange doubts. . . .
And so we come to perceive that the thoughts of these
friends walking to the village near Jerusalem, were in
all essentials like the thoughts of many friends who
are walking to villages near London. They may not
be talking of what happened in the Passion Week. .
. . But they may be asking each other gloomily and
despairingly, whether all the hopes they had once cherished of something better and nobler for the world
and for themselves have not been scattered: whether
friends to whom they looked up have not gone out of
their sight or failed to fulfil their promises; whether
the tidings they heard in their childhood of a Revelation to man, and a Redemption to men, have not lost
their meaning and power. How many are living now
with this weight on their hearts. How many show by
their speech and their looks that they are sad!

We are told that circumstances have changed. .
. . Doubtless, the saying is true; circumstances are
always changing; but the necessities of man's being

do not change. What was true of man generations
ago, is true now.

***

A man will not be really intelligible to you, if, instead of listening to him and sympathizing with him,
you determine to classify him.

***

At what point the strong conviction of a truth which
must be divine, which must be given us from above,
becomes mixed with self-exaltation, with the desire of
showing how wise we are, and of exercising a dominion
over others for our own sakes, it is hard to determine
in any case. The more we know of ourselves, the
more we shall understand how it is possible to vibrate
between the certainty we have of principles, which
for the sake of our moral being we cannot part with,
and a positiveness about notions which we have
grounded upon them. When the conscience is clear,
when the man is lowly, when he has been subdued by
discipline, the opposition seems clear to him as between
day and night; the delusion of his own heart is manifested to him by the light which God has kindled
there. But amidst the noise of human applause the
distinction which was so definite vanishes, the precious
and the vile become hopelessly mingled. Such personal
experiences, which all have had in a greater or less
degree . . . may help us to read the biographies

of men who have had a great influence upon the world, with a kindlier and truer feeling. Their impressions were, doubtless, more overpowering than ours, their conflicts greater, their temptations severer. It is hard to say that, because they called themselves inspired, they meant to deceive; that language might be the language of humility, not of arrogance. . . . Not in this conviction, but in that pride which forgets God — in the desire to be something in themselves — do we trace the beginning of all imposture.

A teacher may, indeed, exercise a much greater power by reviving what is old than by inventing what is new; but to revive a principle, he must have been penetrated by it, it must have taken possession of him, it must have inspired his whole being: otherwise he could never impart it to others. Something of this sort must have been the case with Mahomet.

*_**

In the seventh century after Christ, Mahomet claims to be called of God to a work. We may believe that in many points he greatly mistook the nature of this call, of this work. But the principle that any man who rouses the heart of a nation, who proclaims any deep truth in the midst of it, has a calling — a calling from God — that he has no right to deny it or explain it away; that he cannot do what he is meant to do except on the faith of it; this is a conviction which we Christians, like the Mahometan, have inherited, or ought to have inherited from the Jew.

There is, no doubt, in some persons a very wonderful apprehension and divination of that which others are thinking, imagining, purposing. Those who really have that gift, — who do not merely fancy they have it and make all kinds of false, suspicious, and ill-natured guesses about their neighbors — we call men and women of genius. Sympathy has much to do with genius, perhaps is the essence of it. But it cannot exist, I apprehend, except in a person who has a lively consciousness of what is passing in *him*. He is awake to that, and so can make more than a guess at what is passing in me. . . . The act of conscience is an act in me. It means "I ought, or I ought not." I may pass judgment on other men's acts; but that is another process; I am abusing terms and what the terms represent if I identify it with the conscience.

The distinction of the civilized man from the savage is, as it seems to me, that he is not, to the same extent, the victim of external influences, that he rises above them and tries to rule them. The external authority of the parent or teacher, I maintain, is useless unless

he appeals to that which is within the child, is mischievous unless it is exerted to call that forth. The
external authority must become an internal authority,
not co-operating with the forces which are seeking to
crush the *I* in the child but working against those
forces, working to deliver the child from their dominion. The punishments therefore which are the weapons of this authority . . . must be directed expressly
to *this* purpose. . . . If the child is taught to
have a dread of (the teacher) as one who is an inflicter
of pain, not to have a reverence for him as one who
cares for it, and is seeking to save it from its own folly
— if the child is instructed carefully to separate the
pain arising out of its own acts from the pain which
he inflicts, so that it may associate the pain with him
rather than with them — then all has been done which
human art can do to make it grow up a contemptible
coward, crouching to every majority which threatens
it with the punishments that it has learnt to regard as
the greatest and only evils ; one who may at last . .
. become the spontaneous agent of a majority in
trampling out in others the freedom which has been
so assiduously trampled out in him. A parent or a
teacher who pursues this object is of all the ministers
of a community the one whom it should regard with
the greatest abhorrence, seeing that he is bringing up
for it, not citizens, but slaves.

*
* *

There are grave doubts among men of the world
whether the student of morals has any real subject to
treat of. He can talk much about the blessings of
virtue and the mischiefs of vice. But Lord Macaulay,
who spent a great part of his life in dealing with virtues and vices as a legislator, or in recording the effects
of them as a historian, said . . . that the most
brilliant writer upon them did not deserve half the
gratitude from mankind which is due to the maker of
a substantial pair of shoes.

*
* *

. . . To the Buddhist, the belief in God is the
most awful, and at the same time the most real, of all
thoughts; one not thrust back into the corner of a
mind which is occupied by everything else, but which
he thinks demands the highest and most refined exercise of all the faculty that he has. It is something
which is to make a change in himself, which is at once
to destroy him and to perfect him. And the effect is
a practical one. Buddha is ever at rest. Can his
worshipper be turbulent? Can he admit any rude or
violent passions into his heart? He must cultivate
gentleness, evenness, all serene and peaceful qualities,
reverence and tenderness to all creatures, or he is not
in his rightful state. He is not tempted, or obliged,
as the Brahmin is, to look upon any human creature as

merely animal, as excluded even from the highest privileges. . . . The poorest man of the vilest race may become one with Buddha. Hence, though he belongs to no priestly family, all his functions are more essentially those of a priest than a Brahmin's can be. He claims no civil distinction; he is to be reverenced simply as offering up prayers for the peace and prosperity of all other people.

It is no doubt true that a man who follows his own notions and vagaries may be as far from the laws of the universe as the man who accepts all the traditions of other days. But those who, under pretence of hindering notions and vagaries, try in any degree to forbid or discourage the exercise of men's thoughts in reference to these laws, are laboring that they may be always hidden. The laws may reveal themselves to any seeker if he be ever so blundering a one. They will not reveal themselves to any one who is content with his own opinions and does not wish to change them for truth. It is a reasonable assertion that any man who interferes with these investigations, is an enemy of the Liberty of Conscience.

We have seen that the Brahm of the Hindoo, the Buddha of that mighty sect which arose out of Hin-

dooism, is especially the Intelligent Being, He in whom
light dwells, and by communication with whom men
become enlightened.　Observe how naturally, how inevitably, one uses this word Light for Intelligence.
We feel instinctively that it is much the better word
of the two. . . . So men have felt in all countries
and ages.　Their bodily eye distinguished one thing
from another.　They had as certainly something within
them which could discern a sense in words, a meaning
in things.　This surely was an eye too. . . . And
there must be some light answering to this eye, older
than it, otherwise it could not be.　They discovered,
too surely also, that there was a state in which this
eye saw nothing, a state of darkness.　If we keep
these very simple thoughts in our minds, . . . and
if we recollect that what we are apt to overlook as too
simple is oftentimes just the most important thing of
all — the key which unlocks a multitude of treasure-
houses — we shall be able to enter into the belief of
different people, and to trace the transition from one
to another far more easily.

When I ask for the secret of that specially real and
practical character which all ages have concurred in
attributing to Socrates, I find it in his Egotism.　I
might give you instances of what I mean from either
of his disciples, but Xenophon's testimony in this case

at least might be more suspected. He was a soldier
and a man of business; when he speaks of Socrates as
practical, we might fancy he gave his master credit for
the quality which he preferred to all others, and which
he had acquired in the world. . . . The passage
which I shall choose from (Plato) is taken from one
of his most poetical dialogues; it occurs at the beginning of the Phaedrus. Socrates and Phaedrus are sitting near the spot from which Boreas was reported to
have carried off the nymph Oreithyia. Socrates has
heard such explanations; they are ingenious; he ad-
mires the cleverness of those who invented them. But,
if he resorts to this kind of interpretation for the
story of Boreas, he must treat Gorgons, Centaurs,
Chimaeras, after the same fashion. . . . "And my
friend," he says, "I cannot find leisure for it. I have
not yet complied with the precept of the oracle; I am
not yet able to know myself. It seems to me ridicu-
lous whilst I am in this ignorance to busy myself with
subjects which lie at a distance from me." . . .
Here is the Egotist. And here is the practical man
we have all heard of. He who could dismiss all questions about Boreas and Oreithyia that he might settle
accounts with himself . . . might indeed be said
to bring philosophy out of the cloud-land to the *terra
firma*. . . . Nor can we wonder at the power
which he had of attracting men, especially young men,

to him, or at the bitter hostility which he provoked. There is no attraction in general formulas and propositions; there is an immense charm in one, however uncouth in his appearance, who can enter into desires and perplexities, which he has first realized in his own life, and through which he has fought his way. There is no terror in mere propositions and formulas, there is great terror in one who arouses us to remember that which we would rather forget; he would take from us the Lethe cup; we may be willing that he should drain the cup of hemlock.

*_**

Epictetus has sent down to us not his groans, but his thanksgivings, that he was not bound to be a slave such as he perceived Nero was; that, being Epictetus, he might enjoy freedom, if he did not cast it away. For this he said was slavery, to be the victim of the representations made to the senses, — of all the impressions which we receive from without. To this ignominious state of bondage Nero was reduced. Able to command all pleasures, able to decline all pains, the poor man was the passive victim of the things about him; he was sinking lower and lower under their dominion; he was less and less able to assert himself. If Epictetus was a slave, submission to these impressions, not the power of a master to send him to the mines or to inflict chastisement upon him, was the cause of his slavery. If he did not fasten the chains upon himself, no one else could put them on him; he had the key of the prison doors.

**

The Meditations of Marcus Aurelius exhibit a man who is striving by all means that he knows of — by the help of old traditions, of family attachments, of one or another form of Greek wisdom — to recover something which he feels has departed, or is departing from his country, from those who are governing in it, from those who are serving in it. The greatness of a battle conducted under such circumstances I cannot appreciate; if I dared speak of it in the language of some as a wonderful effort of unassisted reason, I contradict my faith. . . I believe the conscience and reason of Marcus Aurelius could not have been called forth — as I believe yours and mine cannot — by any less Divine Teacher than the one whom he confessed, but knew not how to name.

**

(Marcus Aurelius Antoninus) wrote in Greek; he dwelt in all the effeminacy of a Court. But he desired above all things, he says, to be a male and a Roman. What he meant by that we can understand from his acts, and also from his thoughts; for he is one of those who has let us look into the secrets of his life; who has told us what he was striving to be, and what helps and hindrances he met with in his strivings. **He had evidently** taken account of the causes which **had made** the Roman a ruler of the world. He had seen that self-restraint had been one main secret of **his power;** that reverence for the relations in which he found himself had been another. Out of both had come the habit of obedience; that obedience was involved in the oath of the soldier; that obedience was the only security for the fidelity of the citizen.

* *

. . . Cicero's character is a complicated one, hard to describe faithfully upon a single hypothesis, capable of being contemplated on various sides, supplying plentiful excuses for a severe criticism as well as for cordial admiration. Since he was the man who was most perfectly seasoned in Greek literature of all his cotemporaries; since he was at the same time essentially Latin in thoughts, language, affections, character, and regarded all his Greek culture as ornamental and subsidiary; since, nevertheless, he has taken more pains to show us how it might, in his judgment, be helpful to the main object of the Roman's life; — he must be the best illustration we can find, both in his person and his writings, of the whole subject. His vanity belongs to himself; his political oscillations, and his domestic failures, much more to his time; the uncertainty of his conclusions, to his education both in the schools and at the bar. But beneath all these there lies the Roman reverence, the Roman sense of duty, the Roman tenderness and affection, and, I must add, laying stress upon the adjective, the *Roman* love of truth. That love of truth was altogether distinct from the Greek love of it. Truth in itself Cicero did not pursue or care for, or know the meaning of. But truth in institutions, truth in character, truth in the ordinary dealings of men, he did admire very heartily, even if various influences to the right and to the left made him deviate often and sadly from his standard.

* *

Napoleon the First, when about fifteen years of age, was in the military school at Paris. He complained to the superintendents of the school about its arrangements. What do you suppose were his objections to them? He said the fare of himself and his brother scholars was too luxurious. It could not prepare them for living in poor households, still less for the hardships of the camp. He urged that, instead of having two courses a day, they should have ammunition bread and soldiers' rations and that they should be compelled to mend and clean their own stockings and shoes. Here you have a young Ascetic. . . He chose what was painful in preference to what was pleasant. And because he did so, he was able hereafter to trample upon those peoples and monarchs who ac-

counted pleasure the end of life, whose greatest desire
was to avoid pain.· No Alpine snows, no armed men
could withstand him.   Only when he encountered
men, who had learned, as he had learned, to claim dominion over circumstances, to endure suffering for the
sake of a higher end, could that strength, which he
had won through his Asceticism, be broken. Napoleon
was no theorist, he hated theories.   He wanted to
be independent of his own inclinations that he might
exercise power over other men.   The stoical *theory*
was deduced from an observation, how much power a
man possesses who is not the victim of pleasures or of
pains.

**

Liberty of Conscience cannot mean liberty to *do* what
I like. That we have seen, in the judgment of the
wisest men, of those who speak most from experience,
is bondage. It is from my likings that I must be
emancipated if I would be a free-man. It cannot
mean liberty to *think* what I choose. Such men as
Marcus Aurelius discovered the slavery which came
from thinking what they chose, the necessity of bringing their thoughts under government lest they should
become their oppressors. Every teacher of physical
Science . . . repeats the same lesson. The scientific man bids us seek the thing as it is. He tells us
that we are always in danger of putting our thoughts

or conceptions of the thing between us and that which is. He gives us a discipline for our thoughts that they may not pervert the facts which we are examining. .
. . When Galileo said to those who condemned him, " And yet the earth does move," he said, " Neither my thoughts nor the thoughts of all the doctors and priests that live now or ever have lived can the least alter facts. You have no right, I have no right, to determine what is. All our determinations must fall before the truth when that is discovered to us."

III.

REFORMS.

To assert a divine true Fatherhood in place of the paternal tyrannies which have counterfeited it, must, I conceive, be the work of those who would educate and civilize the nations in the way in which they never have been educated and civilized, and never can be by those who merely seek, even with the utmost skill, to cultivate their material prosperity, at the expense of their inward life.

**

We have . . . never doubted that the whole country must look for its blessings through the elevation of the Working Class, that we must all sink if that is not raised. We have never dreamed that that class could be benefited, by losing its working character, by acquiring habits of ease, or self-indulgence. We have rather thought that *all* must learn the dignity of labor and the blessing of self-restraint. We could not talk to suffering men of intellectual or moral improvement, without first taking an interest in their physical condition and their ordinary occupations; but we felt that any interest of this kind would be utterly wasted, that it would do harm and not good, if it were not the means of leading them to regard themselves as human beings made in the image of God.

*
* *

. . . A multitude of . . . influences . . . are tending to make Work not that brave noble occupation of men's hands which is so beneficial to the labor and the rest of their minds, but a feverish effort to produce quickly that which may look well, and be puffed largely, and be sold at a low rate, to the great loss of the purchaser. The sense of responsibility which led the Greek to be as diligent in working out that part of the statue which would be hidden by the wall of the temple as that part which would be exposed to the eye, because the gods would look upon both, seems to have departed from Christendom, which should cherish it most.

*
* *

That all the gifts which any have received through one instrumentality or another, all general knowledge, all professional knowledge — and that which we may be rich in if we are poor in these, experience of our own failures and errors, of the wrongs we have done, of the good we have missed — should be turned to the

service of that class which is, indeed, not a class, but
which represents the stuff of humanity after class distinctions have been removed from it — in which lie the
germs of the worst evil, and of the best good that is in
any of the classes — *the Working-men* — this is the
doctrine that I have maintained in the Lectures on
Learning and Working.

* *

We must learn . . . that the order of society,
like the order of nature, was not created by us for our
convenience, and cannot shape itself according to our
convenience : that we are all its subjects; that it
asserts itself; that it avenges itself : that we are hum-
bly and devoutly to ask what its demands upon us are,
and whence we can obtain the power of fulfilling them.
Then when we have received a little of this wisdom
. . . we may be able to raise our working people out of some of the delusions to which they, as well
as we, are prone. We may lead them to perceive,
since we shall first have perceived it ourselves, that
obedience is not hard and servile compulsion; that
politics are not created in conformity to certain theories of ours: . . . that every piece of machinery, —
that the commonest acts of those who use machinery;
— indicate the divine laws to which the sun and stars
do homage.

**

The bodily energies being given to man by his Creator, and being liable to all abuse — the senses being given to man by his Creator, and being liable to all abuse — no education can be sound and true which makes light of either, which does not treat the development of them as a solemn duty, not merely as a bye work.

**

What we want to make working men feel is that the ordinary business of life is compatible with — nay, is in strictest harmony with — the best and highest knowledge. They have been almost utterly separated in their minds, to a great extent they have been separated in ours: our business is, to reconcile them in both.

**

Oh! let us give over our miserable notion that poor men only want teaching about things on the surface, or will ever be satisfied with such teaching! They are groping about the roots of things whether we know it or not. You must meet them in their underground search, and show them the way into daylight, if you want true and brave citizens, not a community of dupes and quacks.

**

. . . . We have found an unbelief in the authority of the Bible very common among the working-men:

we have found infidel notions of all kinds prevailing among them; we have found these notions gaining immense strength from the notion that the Scripture refers to a future world and not to the present. Our great object has been to encounter this infidelity by showing them that the Bible, taken in its most simple literal sense, declares God to be the present ruler of the world, and that, if they have faith in Him and in His word, they will find a help and a teacher in their daily perplexities, in their common life, which will save them from resorting to demagogues as ignorant as themselves.

There is a kind of Christianized teaching about philology, history, physiology, which seems to me most unchristian. It is offensive to the scientific man, because it twists facts to a moral; to the devout man, because it treats the laws of God's universe and His acts as less sacred than our inferences from them; to the workingman, because he asks us to help him to see the truth of things, and he thinks we are plotting to deceive him. If you regard Christianity as something which is to be spread and sprinkled over the surface of things, to prevent truth from being dangerous — if you have not courage to look into the roots of knowledge and science, because you are sure that the God of truth and righteousness is there — you had better leave the workingman alone, unless you desire to make him a thousand times more of an infidel than you give him credit for being already.

**

God's order seems to me more than ever the antagonist of man's system ; Christian Socialism is in my mind the assertion of God's order. Every attempt, however small and feeble, to bring it forth, I honor and desire to assist. Every attempt to hide it under a great machinery, call it Organization of Labor, Central Board, or what you like, I must protest against as hindering the gradual development of what I regard as a divine purpose, as an attempt to create a new constitution of Society, when what we want is that the old constitution should exhibit its true functions and energies.

**

To set trade and commerce right we must find some ground, not for them, but for those who are concerned in them, for men to stand upon.

**

I am most thankful to be able to connect Church Reformation with social Reformation — to have all one's thoughts tested by their application to actual work and by their power of meeting the wants of suffering, discontented, resolute men. Whatever will not stand that trial is not good for much. I am sure that all which is of God in my desires and methods will: that what is my own will be exposed and cast out as it ought to be.

* *

The good master . . . is the one who allows least influence to the principle of competition in determining his own acts towards the workmen, and the one who is most careful that he shall rule competition, making it, as he says, a competition for excellence, instead of cheapness, and that competition shall not rule him. I accept the definition and fully believe that the more encouragement we give to the principle of association, the more of such masters we shall form. . . . I apprehend that every successful strike tends to give the workmen a very undue and dangerous sense of their own power, and a very alarming contempt for their employer, and that every unsuccessful strike drives them to desperate and wild courses. In urging them to direct their passion for association, which can never cease among them and is just now especially rampant, into a different channel, I think we are favoring the cause of order, diminishing the rage against capital, and helping the manufacturers much more than they will help themselves if they merely raise a wild cry against Socialism.

* *
*

If great commercial enterprises require the co-opera-
tion and predominance of the capitalist, as I am not
at all disposed to deny that they do, then the capitalist
will find his proper field. He will be obliged, I believe, in due time, to admit his workmen to a share of
his profits, but I question exceedingly whether he will
find those workmen at all disposed to controvert his
judgment about the best way of realizing ultimate ad-
vantages, if he gives them an adequate support com-
mensurate to their services, such support, of course, to
be deducted from their future gains. In the meantime, so far as I can observe, the workmen are most
glad, only too glad, to defer to the intelligent and experienced capitalist if they see that he has their interest at heart as well as his own.

* *
*

What I have tried to say is that the reorganizers of
society and the conservators of society are at war,
because they start from the same vicious premisses;
because they tacitly assume lands, goods, money, labor,
some subjects of possession, to be the basis of society
and therefore wish to begin by changing or maintaining
the conditions of that possession: whereas, the true
radical reform and radical conservation must go much
deeper and say: Human relations not only should lie,
but do lie beneath all these, and when you substitute

— upon one pretext or another — property relations for these . . . you introduce hopeless anarchy.

. . . We have tried to teach the workingmen in our words what we have tried to show them in our acts — that Christianity is the only means of promoting their well-being, and counteracting the moral evils which lie at the root of their physical evils. . . . We have protested against the spirit of competition and rivalry precisely because we believe it is leading to anarchy, and must destroy at last the property of the rich as well as the existence of the poor.

There is certainly an impression abroad, which is shared by some of the most zealous supporters of popular education, that our schools for the poor . . . are not bringing up helpful, intelligent workers, that, from some accident or other, their learning and work stand altogether apart from each other, so that the best scholar may sometimes almost seem to have had the faculties dulled and stunted which he needs for the toils in which he must be engaged. If this is the case, we ought to know it and confess it. . . . We ought freely to admit that any education which fails to make poor men or rich men efficient in action, is an unsatisfactory education — one which needs to be reformed, not only for the sake of its results, but because the studies which produce such results cannot themselves be sincere and wholesome.

Amongst us, more than amongst our fathers of the last century, the questions are debated, How are we to educate ourselves, how are we to educate men and women and children of different classes, from the highest to the lowest? Till we determine what we are, what there is in these men and women and children which can be educated, till we settle whether we are to be treated and are to treat others as atoms of a mass, or whether each of us is a distinct I, and must be taught to believe that he is so and to act as if he were, I cannot conceive that we shall make much advance in the Science of Education.

It will avail nothing to offer prizes to men of all conditions: such a scheme may create a race of nimble clerks, it will form no seers and statesmen; — if you do not set before the people of England some standard of worth such as no prizes ever taught them to contemplate, — if you do not offer them some sincere knowledge, such as prizes often tempt them to exchange for what is most glossy and superficial. Let

the skilful quill-driver have his reward . . . but,
if we want to create heroes, or to save them from per-
ishing when we have them, let those who used to boast
that they existed to form English gentlemen, show
that their occupation is not gone; only that they believe gentleness is not tied to wealth, not even to
birth; that God can cultivate it and would cultivate
it, in the collier and street-sweeper.

. . . Those who think most earnestly of infant
education must think of adult education. . . . They
cannot expect to teach infants by infants. They must
above all things desire that the mothers should have
wise, loyal, English hearts. By all means let us labor
for that end. If I did not believe that the education
of workingmen would lead us by the most direct road
to the education of working-women, I should care
much less for it.

What we want is not to put things into our pupils'
minds so much as to set in order what we find there,
to untie knots, to disentangle complicated threads. .
. . If there be in every artisan the seeds of all the
theories of morals that have ever existed in the world;
if you see these seeds bearing fruit in different parts
of his practice; if he is the selfish man and the be-

nevolent man, the idealist and the pursuer of compro-
mises, the seeker of pleasure and the sufferer of pain
a hundred times in the same week ; then I know nothing more interesting, or that may be more useful than
to follow out these different tracks. . . . The
effort presumes some knowledge of what is going on
in the minds of our pupils and in our own, together
with a sense that it is very fragmentary, and needs to
be increased by intercourse with them and with ourselves. It presumes, also, that we have sufficient faith
in what we have hold of, to be willing that it should
be subjected to all possible tests. . . . Like all
efforts, it must be attended with much humiliation ;
but then what a reward !

A teacher may give the most cordial welcome to the
convictions and hopes which he will find stirring in
the hearts of the workingmen, and yet may bring the
experience of history to remove their prejudices and
diminish their asperities. This cannot be, if we do
not come to the task with a willingness to have our
own theories broken to pieces by facts; desirous to
find men better than we have supposed them to be;
determined to show that what is right and true must
be mightier and must show itself to be mightier than
we and all other men are.

**
* **

The more we look upon man as a spiritual being, the more we regard education as intended to bring forth his spirit, the more we shall desire to train his animal nature and his senses, because they will certainly enslave his spirit, if they are not made its servants.

**
* **

We certainly believe that the Socialism which Mr. Southey and other eminent Conservatives accepted as a solution of some of the greatest practical difficulties of England, if it were based upon Christianity, might be the most powerful protection of the land against anarchical notions and practices, whether taking the name of Socialism or adopted as precautions against it. We have formed small associations among workingmen for the carrying on of their own trades, in which the Sunday is a day of rest, intemperance is checked, political agitation is discouraged. We know that, by so doing we have led some workmen to see the folly and danger of strikes. . . .

**
* **

Competition is put forth as the law of the universe. That is a lie. The time is come for us to declare that it is a lie by word and deed. I see no way but associating for work instead of for strikes. I do not say or think we feel that the relation of employer and em-

ployed is not a true relation. I do not determine that
wages may not be a righteous mode of expressing that
relation. But at present it is clear that this relation is
destroyed, that the payment of wages is nothing but a
deception. We may restore the whole state of things;
we may bring in a new one. God will decide that.
His voice has gone forth clearly bidding us come
forward to fight against the present state of things.

* *

. . . Almost any risk should be incurred . . .
for the sake of making the laborers understand that
citizenship is a reality, that civilization is not a curse,
that the same power which enabled their forefathers
to work together in spite of all the tendencies to solitude and rivalship in the fourteenth century, can enable them to overcome the same tendencies, in the
more fortunate circumstances of the nineteenth. . .
. The principle of Trade is reciprocity, not overreach-
ing.

* *

My principle is good for nothing if it depends upon
social accidents, if it is not as valid for those who pay
wages as for those who claim the fealty of vassals.
Family Relations last on through all changes: I claim
the Relation of Master and Servant as one of these. .
. . I rejoice in all those facts which prove that the
Servant has a legal status: that he has as much claim

against his Master in the Courts as his Master has against him. . . . But I am sure that unless (Master and Servant) learn that reverence for each other which neither feudal bonds nor legal securities can create, they will become more and more enemies to each other.

*_**

The greatest good of all to Law, Physic, and Divinity, may be expected, as I think, if lawyers, physicians and divines, determine in their hearts that the hand workers shall not be mere drudges more than themselves, that they also shall be taught how to work as men, that they shall have such Freedom and such an Order as no arrangements of society, without a spirit to direct them and the men who compose the society, can ever give.

If . . . we are consistent with our own habitual professions, we must aim in all our teaching of the working classes, at making them free. We know that they feel themselves shackled in a thousand ways: that they ask to be delivered from their shackles. They may be wrong in some of their notions about the *nature* of their bondage; they are not wrong about the *fact* of it. If you think that it is upon their souls, and not upon their bodies, then you will set about emancipating their souls. If the distinction between a freeman and a slave, as Mrs. Stowe has taught us, . . . is identical with the distinction between a **Person** and a **Thing**, you will seek above all things to make our working people understand that they are Persons, and not Things.

**

I have often felt as if the phrases "manly education" — "education for men" — which I have used so often in these Lectures, must have an offensive sound, as if I were devising a teaching which should be confined to one sex. But I have adopted these phrases deliberately, being certain that, by employing them, I am doing my best to vindicate a high education for women. Where the education of men is not manly — where it is effeminate — they will always be disposed to degrade their wives and sisters; they will always be suspicious of their rivalry. When it has been most masculine — as in Queen Elizabeth's days — the culture of women has been free and noble in the same proportion.

**

I do not know any man who has seriously thought of our present examination system who does not feel that it is undermining the physical, intellectual and moral life of young men, and that it may do this with even more terrible effect for girls, if they are admitted, as of course they should be, to all the privileges of the other sex. . . . You must know well that noble intellects, which crave for a free culture, are dwarfed by the notion that what they have read and thought is not to be tested and ascertained by the questions of wiser men, but that they are to read and think simply with a view to the questions.

No one, I believe, knows the extent of confusion and perplexity which there is in the minds of young men at the present day, nor the little hope they have of coming out of it, nor their readiness to turn anywhere for the help which they cannot find among divines. Would that I could speak what I feel sometimes is in me; but it must come out in acts more than words, and God can find other and better instruments, and I am sure will.

. . . When we have got rid of these confused notions which have fastened themselves to the cry for Liberty of Conscience, there remains a most wholesome and indispensable protest in it to which no Statesmen or Churchmen or Philosophers can be indifferent except at their great peril. The opinion has prevailed among all three that the Conscience is a troublesome disturber of the peace, which it may be necessary to endure, but which it would be very desirable to silence. So long as that doctrine prevails, so long as any frag-

ment or shred of it remains in our minds, we may talk
about persecution as much as we please: we may boast
of our age for having discovered the inutility of persecution; but we shall, under one pretext, or other, fall
back upon it. . . . What satisfactory demonstrations
there will be that we are really vindicating toleration
when we are most intolerant, that we are not interfering
with a man's belief, but only with his desire to crush
ours! Therefore I deem it needful to proclaim that in
every instance to which we can point, a Society which
has succeeded in choking or weakening the Conscience
of any of its members has undermined its own existence, and that the defeat of such experiments has been
the preservation and security of the Society that has
attempted them.

**
* **

I have the best reason to know that the minds of
numbers in all classes of society — of young men, especially, — are unsettled, not on some trifling or secon-
dary questions, but on those which affect their inmost
faith and their practical conduct, on those which concern the character of God and their relations to Him.
. . . I have maintained . . . that there is no
safety but in looking fairly in the face all the difficulties which beset ourselves; but in frankly meeting all
the difficulties which torment our brethren; that God
encourages us to do this; that by doing it we show

that we trust Him to give us the help which He has
promised us, a help which can deliver us from falsehood and guide us into all truth.

⁎⁎

Weaker men may be crushed under the thought of
what it is which the greatest number require and how
they are ever to attain what they require.   But if they
are driven in their despair to think that there is One
who knows this better than they do — if that is the
only belief in which they are able to work for their
fellow-men — they cannot be otherwise than grateful
to (Mr. Bentham) for suggesting the aim which they
own that they are quite unable to reach, (by his
" *Greatest Happiness of the greatest number.*")   It is
not, indeed, in a comfortable Optimism that they can
ever find refuge from the palpable evils which he has
set before them or from the sense of their own im-
potence.   Those who have ever *wished* for the greatest happiness of a majority of their race or of the
whole of it, cannot acquiesce in any pleasant dreams
that somehow it will drop upon them from the skies.
They know that it is better to be miserable than to
take up with a lie : that nothing is so miserable as a
lie.   The service Mr. Bentham will have done them is
in leading them to ask themselves whether there is not
a *Truth* in which the greatest number of men — in
which all men — may trust, and whether that *Truth*

will not make them free. If there is a Happiness
without Freedom, or beyond it, they may wait to learn
what that is.

The fact is, that there is that in every man which calls
out for salvation from drunkenness : there is a man
within him who wants another life, and who at the same
time confesses his incapacity to rise to that higher life.
. . . If you speak to the human being in him, I do
not say that he will understand you. It may be a
long time before you get to understand him, or he,
you. But I do say that the message of God's kingdom, the message of eternal life, will reach him as no
message about happiness ever will.

We want for the establishment and rectification of
our Social Morality not to dream ourselves into some
imaginary past or some imaginary future, but to use
that which we have, to believe our own professions,
to live as if all we utter when we seem to be most in
earnest were not a lie. Then we may find that the
principle and habit of self-sacrifice which is expressed
in the most comprehensive human Worship supplies
the underground for national Equity, Freedom, Courage ; for the courtesies of common intercourse, the
homely virtues and graces which can be brought under
no rules, but which constitute the chief charm of life,

and tend most to abate its miseries.   Then every
tremendous struggle with ourselves whether we shall
degrade our fellow-creatures, men and women, or live
to raise them — struggles to which God is not indifferent if we are, — may issue in a real belief that we are
members one of another, and that every injury to one
is an injury to the whole body.   Then it will be found
that refinement and grace are the property of no class,
that they may be the inheritance of those who are as
poor as Christ and His Apostles were: because they
are human.   So there will be discovered beneath all
the politics of the Earth, sustaining the order of each
country, upholding the charity of each household, a City
which has foundations, whose builder and maker is God.
It must be for all kindreds and races ; therefore, with the
sectarianism which rends Humanity asunder, with the
Imperialism which would substitute for Universal Fellowship, a Universal Death, must it wage implacable
war.   Against these we pray as often as we ask that
God's will may be done in Earth as it is in Heaven.

IV.

BOOKS.

. . . Some books exhibit very transparently what sort of a person he was who wrote them; they show *him* to us. I think we shall find that there is the charm of the book, the worth of the book. . . . There is a man who writes, and, when you get acquainted with that man, you get acquainted with the book. It is no more a collection of letters and leaves: it is a *friend*.

**
*

I always tell my pupils not to read cold, impartial biographies, but to study a man's life in the book of some one who loved him.

**
*

I do not know any one who makes us feel more than Milton does, the grandeur of the ends which we ought to keep always before us, and therefore our own pettiness and want of courage in pursuing them. . . . I would rather converse with him as a friend than talk

103

of him as a poet; because then we put ourselves into
a position to receive the best wisdom which he has to
give us, and that wisdom helps to purge away whatever dross is mingled with it; whereas, if we merely
contemplate him at a distance as a great genius, we
shall receive some powerful influence from him, but
shall not be in a condition to compare one thing that
he says to us with another. And to say the truth, I
do not know what genius is, except it be that which
begets some life in those who come in contact with it,
which kindles some warmth in them.

***

Shakespeare has taught us not to choose out dainty
bits of our own national records and to feed exclu-
sively on them. He has shown us that any period, the
most apparently flat and dull, the most turbulent and
bewildering, contains its lesson and will give out that
lesson if we deal fairly with it, and do not force it
into conformity with our own notions.

***

Whatever we may think of Shakespeare's Plays as
guides to a knowledge of English History, I think
most people will confess that they have learnt more
about the different people who have acted in that history from them than from any other source. The men
and women whom he shows us are not names or shadows, but such as we at once recognize, such as we are

sure must have been. . . . The titles of his plays
are not chosen unfairly or by accident. He does not
put King John, King Richard II., King Henry IV. in
the front of the battle, and then exhibit to us some of
the more striking events, or the more remarkable people of their times. The kings are the prominent figures in the drama; the others all stand in some relation
to them.

**
* *

Do you remember what Charles Lamb says about
his wanting a grace before Shakespeare and Milton as
well as a grace before meat? I am sure this is true if
our books are not to choke us.

**
* *

Chaucer is the genuine specimen of an English poet
—a type of the best who were to come after him:
with cordial affection for men and for nature: often
tempted to coarseness, often yielding to his baser nature in his desire to enter into all the different experiences of men: apt through this desire, and through
his hatred of what was insincere to say many things
of which he had need to repent, and of which he did
repent; but never losing his loyalty to what was pure,
his reverence for what was divine.

**
* *

Why is it that we like to read the poems of a man
who has more of this feeling (susceptibility to the

beauties of Nature) then we have ourselves? Is it not because we look upon him as our spokesman? He brings out something that was hidden in us — that we did not know was in us. He says what we should like to say if we could. He is, then, not a more special man than we are: he is more of a common man. The human sympathies have been more awakened in him than in us.

* *

I do not believe that the interest which we have taken in Scott's poems, or Scott's novels, was owing chiefly to their exhibition of great knights and noble personages, though no doubt that has contributed to their fame. I believe the genial sympathy which he showed with the Scotch people, his Jeanie Deans and Edie Ochiltree, have been the real and permanent strength of his works. To these we turn with ever fresh pleasure; and it is a consolation to reflect that so much genial sympathy could have existed in a man writing during the faded and artificial days of the Regency.

* *

. . . Thomas Fuller, one of the liveliest, and yet, in the inmost heart of him, one of the most serious writers one can meet with. . . . There is no one who is so resolute that we should treat him as a friend, and not as a solemn dictator. By some unexpected jest, or comical turn of expression, he disappoints your purpose of receiving his words as if they were fixed in print, and asserts his right to talk with you, and convey his subtle wisdom in his own quaint and peculiar dialect.

**
**

I have always contended that Plato is quite as practical as Aristotle : nay, that if he is rightly studied as he would have us study him, in connection with the life and purposes of Socrates, he is more practical. But I am sure that Aristotle has excellences of a very high kind which Plato has not.

**
**

Considering that Aristotle is reckoned so great a dogmatist . . . it is marvellous how free he is from the temptations of the mere schoolman, how little he trusts in mere formulas, how every virtue of which he speaks is only a virtue as it becomes formed in a man. . . . In this respect, the comparison of him with Plato, if it is greatly to his advantage, is for us most instructive. The *Republic* teaches us how the noblest student of Humanity, in his eagerness to grasp the Universal, is likely to lose sight of the Particular. In Plato's vast Communism the Family is lost. Aristotle acknowledges it as the very basis of political society : the relations of the household are the germs of the different forms of government.

*
* *

I have never taken up any dialogue of Plato without getting more from it than from any book not in the Bible. I do not think it signifies much where you begin. The attempts to systematise his writings seem to me in general, unfortunate; his own beautiful and wonderful method is contained in each one and any one thoroughly studied is the initiation to the best. . . . Plato is the commentator on Plato, and it is a great mistake, I am sure, to fancy that anyone else can interpret him as well.

*
* *

. . . This is the Scripture, — not merely an inspired book, as we sometimes call it, thinking to pay it great honor — but an actual discovery of God Himself and of His ways with His creatures. If we consider it only as a collection of inspired sentences or oracles, we may accept it as divine, but we shall gradually lose sight both of Him who is speaking in it, and of those by whom and to whom He is speaking; its godliness and its humanity will disappear together. We shall be continually stumbling at one sentence or another, trying to force them into some strange meaning of our own. . . . If we take that other view of the Bible, — the errors, sins, false or imperfect judgments of its best and wisest men will be no scandals to us; we shall accept them as foils which enable us to see His character more clearly, in whom is light and no darkness at all. We shall perceive that men could only apprehend truth just so far as they saw it in Him after whose image they were formed. Every step in the history will be a step into clearer illumination, God showing Himself more fully, that the thoughts and actions of men may be capable of a closer correspondence to His. At the same time, it will be no perplexity to us, but an infinite comfort. . . . The Bible, so considered, becomes an orderly expanding history.

***

The New Testament, I need scarcely tell you, is occupied from first to last — specially the Sermon on the Mount — in showing that acts are nothing except as they are fruits of a state, except as they indicate what the man is, that words are nothing except as they express a mind or purpose.

***

The life of such a Jesus as Renan has described may be written by any one who has learning and artistic skill for the task. The Life of Christ can only be contained in a Gospel of the Kingdom of Heaven.

***

Sometimes we confound a revelation of God with a revelation of certain notions and opinions about God. Sometimes we think that a history of God's revelations

means a history of certain exceptional heroes. Either
of these suppositions is in direct contradiction with
the express language, with the inmost spirit, of the
Bible. God promises to declare Himself to us that we
may believe in Him, trust Him, love Him — not that
we may hold a certain theory concerning Him.

**

Some of the Histories that our age has produced are
books in the truest sense of the word. . . . They
show us what a divine discipline has been at work to
form men; they teach us that there is such a discipline
at work to form us into men. That is the test to
which all books must at last be brought; if they do
not bear it their doom is fixed. They may be light or
heavy, the penny sheet or the vast folio; they may
speak of things seen or unseen; of Science or Art:
. . . they may amuse us, or weary us, flatter us or
scorn us; if they do not assist to make us better and
more substantial men, they are only providing fuel for
a fire larger and more utterly destructive than that
which consumed the Library of the Ptolemies.

**

I am reading Froude's History with great interest
and I hope some profit. After all, how nearly his view
of Henry VIII. accords with that which Shakespeare
got out of the Chronicles by mere intuition. I dare
say it is in the main right. . . . His style is gen-

erally most delightful, far the best historical style for our times that I know, so equable, and free from pretension and jauntiness.

I am glad whenever my books are recognized as real messages by any who have known me. I wish they could always be taken as my efforts after truths which we all want equally, and which I might be better able to reach if I could hear all the doubts and objections which my stammering words raise in honest and earnest minds. They are a kind of fragmentary conversation with known or unknown listeners.

If the newspapers supply us with the material for thinking, they will do us good; if we use them as substitutes for thinking, they will destroy both our intellects and our characters.

All Greek myths and Greek songs have seemed to me very wonderful, not bringing freedom, but expressing the aspiration for it; showing a ladder set up on earth, though lost in the clouds, and reaching to Heaven.

There is no Greek play and no Roman history which may not be connected with what is passing around us.

. . . The more you understand the speech as well as the thoughts of writers, the more you will find that they explain your speech and your thoughts. The more perplexities that entangle you in your practice will be cleared away.

***

Our modern Socialist questions, which must press more and more upon us, will, I conceive, present themselves to you again and again while you are busy with these ancients. And it is a grand thing to read newspapers by their light and them by the light of the newspapers.

***

Dr. Johnson said, and many have said after him, that the reading of " Paradise Lost " is a task which people perform once and are glad never to resume. I do not wonder that this should be so. To have a book put into one's hands which one is told is very sublime, or devout, or sacred, or one of the great epics of the world, is to have a demand made on one's admiration to which we submit at first dutifully, and against which, in a little while, we feel an almost inevitable rebellion. . . . It is quite otherwise, I believe, when we receive it as the deepest, most complete utterance of a human spirit; when it comes forth as the final expression of the thoughts of a man who has been fighting a hard battle, who appears to have been worsted in the battle, who thinks he has fallen on evil days and evil tongues.

*

Milton appears to me greatest when he is on the ground of the Old Testament, comparatively feeble when he ventures into the region of the New Testament. He has been called, and not wrongly, our Hebrew Poet.

*

There is one English religious book, written by a man of the people, by one who had endured all possible anticipations of future misery himself, the habits of whose school would have led him to press them as the most powerful motives on others. The genius of the book has been confessed by scholars: its power has been felt by peasants in this land, and in all lands into the language of which it has been translated, almost since it issued from the writer's gaol. To what is the *Pilgrim's Progress* indebted for this influence? Certainly to the strength with which the feeling of evil, as an actual load, too heavy to be borne, is brought home to its readers. It is the man groaning with the burden upon his back, whom rich and poor sympathize with, whom each recognizes as of his own kindred.

*

Spenser, it seems to me, invented nothing; he took that which he found lying idle and useless and unin-

telligible.   He showed us what sense, and beauty, and
harmony there lay beneath it, what help we may get
from Fairyland, if we understand that Fairyland is
about the noble, and the shopkeeper, and the peasant;
that even in the midst of the city where he was born
a poor man and died, perhaps for lack of bread, there
is a way by which our spirits may ascend into it, may
see its bright skies, and taste its fresh fountains; that
everyone who seeks his armor there, may become as
gentle a knight as he was who wore the Red Cross
shield, may be able to vanquish as many giants and
enchanters as any who went forth from the palace of
Gloriana.

*
* *

The treatise of Milton on Education, . . . whatever may be the merits or mistakes of the plan of
study which it recommends, is one of the most sug-
gestive books ever written, as it is one of the bravest
and noblest; a witness as all his other books are, that
no man has drunk more deeply into the spirit of our
English institutions, if he was over impatient of the
forms, when the spirit as he thought, had departed
from them.

*
* *

It seems to me that we have gone astray in the
study of Scripture, not from excess of simplicity, but
from excess of refinement, from looking to a distance

for that which lies at our feet, from refusing to take
words as they stand, and to believe that the writers
meant what they say they meant.

The Bible itself forces us to ask a multitude of
questions. Because I receive it as a revelation of God,
I am bound to ask what it reveals concerning God.
Because I receive it as a whole book, as a continuous
revelation, I am bound to ask how one part of it accords with and interprets another. We must not fear
to make this demand. It is distrusting the Bible, distrusting God, to have such a fear. And, when we
have not found the answer in any special instance, we
should say so frankly. It cannot shake our faith to
feel such ignorance and confess it.

Looking at the best female literature of our own
and former days, this, as it seems to me, has been its
great function, to claim that all thought shall bear
upon action, and express itself in action, that it shall
not dwell apart in a region of its own.

Dr. Arnold, in an admirable passage of his lectures,
dwells upon the good which he had got from Mitford's
" Greece," not because the sentiments of the historian
were just, or his statements of facts always credible,

but because he wrote in a passion, because he denounced Pericles with the same vehemence with which
he would have denounced Mr. Fox. So Dr. Arnold
learnt that Pericles was not less an actual person, not
more a shadow, than Mr. Fox. . . . We have all
had to bless some one or other for making us know
that we are reading of men and women when we are
reading bound books. I think it is also Dr. Arnold
who says that he owed much to the " Fortunes of
Nigel" for making him recollect that King James
talked broad Scotch. That is the kind of benefit
which we have most of us derived from Sir Walter
Scott. If we cannot always assure ourselves that his
kings and queens, even that his ordinary ladies and
gentlemen, had hearts beneath their robes, we have at
least had one great difficulty removed. They did walk
and talk: they had shoes and head-gear: they are not
only to be found on coins. When we have got them
so far brought into the region of humanity, Shakespeare will show us what they were, as well as what
they wore.

A man should be an artist to write a biography as
much as to write a romance: he will not make the
story of a life intelligible if he has not some knowledge beyond what he derives from the mere statistics
of it.

***

We have here (in the Book of Job) what is at least meant to be a history of human experience. . . . Christendom has received the book in this sense. Doctors have taken pains to illustrate it, and have left it much as they found it. Plain suffering men have understood it with all its difficulties much better than the most simple tracts written expressly for their use. You will see bed-ridden women, just able to make out the letters of it, feeding on it, and finding themselves in it. You will hear men who regard our Theology as a miserable attempt to form a theory of the universe, expressing their delight in this one of our theological books, because it so nobly and triumphantly casts theories of the universe to the ground. How it squares with our hypotheses they cannot imagine, but it certainly answers to the testimony of their hearts.

***

If we have real reverence for Scripture, and a firm belief in that which it declares, we shall never strain a single one of its words or phrases, or strain a single fact to make it fit them. Abstinence from such dishonesty will assuredly bring its reward in clearer apprehensions of the whole record hereafter.

***

There is one memorable passage . . . which belongs solely to St. Matthew. It is that which taught

St. Augustine the difference between the teaching of
Christ and that of the best philosophers: " *Come unto
me, all ye that labor and are heavy laden, and I will
give you rest.*" The words are sufficiently beautiful if
they stood alone, unconnected with the passage imme-
diately preceding. . . . But Augustine can never
have separated them from that sentence. The heavy
burden on his soul was the sense of ignorance of God
and of separation from Him. The philosophers could
awaken this sense, but could not satisfy it when it was
awakened. He who could say that He knew the
Father, and was willing to reveal Him, could say,
" *Come unto me, I will give you rest.*" And He could
then call upon them to take His yoke, to work with
Him in His Father's Kingdom, to become a son lowly
and obedient, as *the* Son was; so to cast off the heavy
oppression of pride and self-will.

⁎

The special calling of St. Matthew seems to be, to
show us the working of the divine power and influence
side by side, with the working of those powers and
influences which counteract it, and the approach of a
crisis which would distinguish and separate them.
Thus the parable of the tares of the field is St. Matthew's. The leaven which the woman hid in three
measures of meal, which recent commentators . . .
have taken to indicate the mixture of an evil and cor-

rupt principle with the pure seed in Christian life and
doctrine, is also his. . . . So that his comparisons
seem especially to bear upon that complete working
out of the mystery of good and the mystery of evil,
which is indicated by the phrase, "end or accomplishment of the age."

A kingship over nature, and over the minds and
bodies of men, is brought out before us by St. Matthew; a life-giving sympathy, an intercourse with the
inner man, a human fellowship, grounded upon, not
contradicting, the divine condescension and compas-
sion, is what St. Luke, more than either of the other
Evangelists, compels us to recognize.

. . . The compilers of our Prayer-Book, living
at the very time when Faith was the watchword of all
parties, thought it wise to introduce the season of
Lent with a prayer and an epistle which declares that
the tongues of men and of angels, the giving all our
goods to feed the poor, the giving our bodies to be
burnt, finally, the faith which removes mountains,
without Charity, are nothing. This Love was to be
the ground of all calls to repentance, conversion, humiliation, self-restraint; this was to unfold gradually
the Mystery of the Passion, and of the Resurrection,

the mystery of Justification by Faith, of the New Life, of Christ's Ascension and Priesthood, of the Descent of the Spirit, of the Unity of the Church. This was to be the induction into the deepest mystery of all, the Name of the Father, and of the Son, and of the Holy Ghost. If it is asked what human charity can have to do with the mysteries of the Godhead, the compilers of the Prayer-Book would have answered, "Certainly nothing at all if human charity is not the image and counterpart of the Divine; if there can be a charity in man . . . unless it was first in God, unless it be the nature and being of God. If He is Charity, . . . Charity will be the key to unlock the secrets of Divinity as well as of Humanity."

⁎

I claim it as the first and noblest distinction of our Prayers, that they set out with assuming God to be a Father, and those that worship Him to be His children. They are written from beginning to end upon this assumption. . . . It confronts you in the first words of the Service; it is so glaring that you almost overlook it; but the further you read, the more earnestly you meditate, the more truly you pray, the more certain you are that it is not only on the surface, but reveals the nature of the soil below. That God is actually related to us in His Son, is the doctrine which is the life of the Prayer-Book.

**

If all Progress consists in the advancing further into light, and the scattering of mists which had obstructed it, the Bible contains the promise of such *Progress*, a promise which has been most fulfilled when it has been most reverently listened to, when men have gone to it with the greatest confidence and hope. I complain of our modern religious world, not for cherishing this confidence or this hope, but for abandoning it and robbing others of it. If we come to the Bible as learners, it has more to teach us yet than we can ask or think. If we believe that we know all that is in it and merely resort to it for sentences and watchwords to confirm our own notions and to condemn our brethren, God will show us — He is showing us — how great the punishment to us and our children must be, for abusing the unspeakably precious treasure with which He has endowed us.

**

. . . If we have sufficient reverence for the Book to follow in the steps which it marks out for us, we may learn something from it. We shall not learn, even then, if we forget that all true words — the truest, most of all — only speak *to* us, when they speak *in* us, when they awaken us to thought, self-questioning, wonder, hope. . . . To imagine that any book, or any living voice can give, if there is not a receiver, or

˙that it can give except according to the measure of
the receiver, is to contradict all experience and all
reason.

The Book of Psalms is the most wonderful book in
the world, because it is the most universal; because in
it saints and seers and prophets and kings prove their
title to their great names, by finding that they have a
greater name still, — that they are men; that they are
partakers in all the poverty, emptiness and sinfulness
of their fellow-creatures; that there is nothing in
themselves to boast of, or claim as their own; that all
which they have is His, who would have all to know
Him and be partakers of His holiness.   And, therefore,
the fifty-first Psalm is, as it seems to me, the real explanation of all the Psalms.   .   .   .

.   .   .   St. John's is not, as some people may care-
lessly imagine, difficult or unintelligible language.   It
is particularly clear and transparent.   We may cloud
it with our conceits, we may interpose a number of
shadows, thrown from ourselves, between it and our
consciences; but, if we will let it bear directly upon
them, they will recognize its force, they will not wait
to have it translated into that which is feebler and more
formal.   To some, the language of symbols may seem

unsatisfactory; some may even denounce it as idola-
trous and profane. . . . But if they will have the
Bible, they must have symbols; they must be content
to let God speak to them through the forms of sense,
because they are His forms, and because no others could
convey His meaning to the hearts which He desires to
take it in, so well as they do.

* *

The Service brings before us on the same day
Psalms written in the most different states of mind,
expressive of the most different feelings. If we have
sympathized in one, it often seems a painful effort to
join in the rest. And so it must, as long as we look
upon prayers and praises as expressions of our moods,
as long as we are not joining in them because we belong to a family and count it our highest glory to lose
ourselves in it and in Him who is the head of it. We
must be educated into that knowledge. It may be
slow in coming, but till it comes, the Psalms are not
intelligible to us; . . . we do not more than half
enter into the parts of the service which we seem to
enter into most. They touch certain chords in our
spirits, but not the most rich and musical chords:
these do not belong to ourselves; they are human;
they answer to the touch of that Divine Spirit who
holds converse with the spirit of a *man* which is
in us.

*
* *

Our private solution (of Scripture) may not be without its use; it may point at one side of a great truth;
but if we idolize it, and set it up against every other,
and search for no farther light, we shall find that we
are ourselves claiming to be higher oracles than those
which we profess to consider divine.

*
* *

In one arrangement concerning these lessons, the
compilers of the Prayer-Book seem to me to have
failed in moral courage. . . . I do not see that
they were justified in omitting the Apocalypse in their
courses of Sunday or daily reading. Had they surrounded it with the solemnities of worship, had they
taught us to read it like the other Scriptures, as if we
were in God's presence, I cannot believe we should
have dared to indulge in the fond trivialities which
every commentator, almost every private individual,
seems to think he may safely pour out on a book surely
as grand and awful as any that exists in human language.

*
* *

No such word (as Christianity) is found in the New
Testament. Surely we may be most thankful for the
omission. For what a vague phrase it is! How continually it stands for a hundred different meanings, or
does duty for a meaning that is absent altogether! It

ıs not Christianity of which the beloved Apostle and all the apostles speak to us; it is Christ. It is not a collection of notions, habits, practices; it is a Person.

***

. . . Truths which the simple and poor in spirit readily apprehend, but which our pride and vanity are perpetually robbing us of, have, I believe, been especially brought home to the hearts of people by the Book of Psalms. Let a man hold his theory about the dictation of Scripture ever so strongly, it must break down with him when he begins to read that book, or at least in any manner to enter into the spirit of it. Is it possible, he must say to himself, that these prayers, these songs, these confessions of sin, were repeated in the ears of a man that he might write them down for the good of the world? . . . Wherever the Psalmist learnt these words, they did come fresh and burning from his heart; they must; or how could they go fresh and burning into other men's hearts? Is it difficult to understand then, how they can have been *inspired*, how God can have been the author of them? Difficult, truly, if we are determined to know what praying, and giving of thanks, and confessing are, without praying and giving of thanks and confessing. Difficult! say, rather, impossible! But, if we have ever tried to perform these acts, tried because we felt we could not live without them; tried with this con-

viction, and yet been disappointed; we do and shall
learn that prayer, if it be man's utterance of his own
wants to God, has yet its beginning and first spring in
Him.

* *

Every subject has so much to do with history, that
every man who is devoted to any subject whose business is mainly with that, has a point of affinity with all
the transactions of his land. . . . The artist, the
tradesman, the student of physics, the soldier, may
each claim his right in the history, may each bring his
contribution to it. Beginning the study from his own
topic, working at it for the sake of that, he finds himself unawares in contact with the friends whose occupations are the most alien from his; he is asking their
help, they are asking his.

* *

If I may judge of others by myself, it is not easy
to express the magnitude of our obligations to Gibbon.
We become more conscious of them the more we en-
deavor to put our thoughts together respecting the
long period which he has described to us, or to consider particular portions of it. We are not only bound
to admire his patient toil, his faithfulness in the study
of documents which a large majority of his contemporaries, and probably of ours, would suppose that he
had no occasion to meddle with, and the power which

he has of awakening our interest in the dullest subjects. These are very great historical gifts; but the
historical genius is more exhibited when a writer en-
ables us to understand that heterogeneous events are
connected, that history is really a drama, every scene
of which has relation to some centre, and is bearing us
on to some issue. The melancholy grandeur of Gibbon's book remains with us and grows deeper as we
look upon any picture of the ruins of Rome, or meditate upon the world that has grown out of them. His
solemn and stately style is felt . . . to be the
proper garb for a funeral procession, such as he brings
before us, and compels us to join. It is a majestic
spectacle to see Greeks and Goths, hordes from the
steppes of Asia which Pompey and Cicero never
dreamed of, the Moors of Africa, nations in all cos-
tumes and of all religions, joining in that procession
and attending the fallen conqueror to his tomb.

**

It has not been a mistake, I believe, in our education,
that we have busied ourselves so much with the legends
of Greece and Rome. If we used them aright, they
would not serve for the food of an idle dilettanteism —
they would teach us reverence and fear. We should
tremble as we remembered, "These dreams of a beauty
which eye hath not seen, nor ear heard, have visited
the hearts of human beings generations ago: the dark

and filthy imaginations which mingled with these
dreams were engendered in the same hearts; by one
as much as the other,   .   .   .   we know that those
hearts are like our own.   They will dwell together in
us, and in time the vile will seem real, the beautiful
only a shadow, unless we can find that the beauty
has been somewhere substantiated ; unless we can see
the beauty apart from the corruption; unless there is
some power which can establish the one and destroy
the other in ourselves."

**
* *

I cannot fall down and worship Nicholas V. or
Lorenzo the Magnificent, or Leo X.   I can as little
bring myself to regret the revival of Latin scholarship
and Greek art, or not to hail it as a very great step
forwards in the divine and moral education of the
West.   I cannot think that a mere dilettanteism and
refinement, which satisfied no one of the great national
impulses that had been awakened in the fourteenth
century, which did nothing whatever for the elevation
of the mind of the people, which scorned the idea of
liberty and popular life, which tolerated the basest
intrigues and the darkest vices, which concealed them,
apologized for them, and allied itself with them; I
cannot conceive that this is a thing which brave men
are bound to admire, or which they can dare to speak
of, as if it had borne any great fruits for mankind.

But on the other hand, I must think that this dilettante-ism, poor and contemptible in itself, was discovering, or at least polishing weapons that were destined to do mighty service for mankind, and partly by working out its own destruction. Call the old literature Classical or Pagan, or what you please, but it was a literature that spoke of national life and energy, of politics that were based upon principles and not upon plots, of statesmen who were first men, of states that were called into being by a divine voice, and which asserted their origin by the vengeance and fall which overtook the human rulers who supposed they could fashion the world at their pleasure. This literature, with all its corruptions, spoke more clearly and distinctly of domestic life as lying at the foundation of civil polity, than any monk, however high his ideal might be, had been able to speak.

***

Can we find no picture . . . which may teach us what the effect upon a man would be if the Conscience were . . . reduced to the smallest possible force and vitality? Modern literature . . . is in this case most helpful. You know the story of Romola . . . and will remember therefore the full length and admirable portrait of the young Greek Tito. With a perception of all sensual delights as exquisite as ever belonged to his race when it was in the fullness

of its glory, with the accomplishments which made it
the teacher of Western Europe in the fifteenth century, with energy for all the intellectual pursuits which
were so dear to the Italians of that day, failing in no
subtlety of mind or grace of person, or aptitude for
affairs, able to attract the admiration of the wisest
statists, and to win the heart of the noblest woman,—
what is there deficient in this man? This only. The
words "I ought" and "I ought not" have vanished
from a vocabulary rich in the spoils of all languages,
capable of expressing every delicate and refined apprehension.

***

(*Romola*) has impressed me very deeply. I think
(George Eliot's) Savonarola is the true man. I have
seldom been more moved than by some of her hints
respecting him in the latter part of the story. And
her Tito, with the exception of his melodramatic exit,
seems to me admirable throughout. Nor can I agree
with Miss Wedgwood in considering Romola a modern
lady. I think she has the dignity and grace at least
of the revived antiquity of her age.

***

Whenever I read *Macbeth* with its blasted heath
and its witch scenery, I feel certain that the story is
essentially true; that no change of circumstances or of
opinions has made it less real, less tremendous for our

time than for the time in which it was composed. .
. . Suggestions do come to a man now as of old
which he dallies with, which mix with dreams of ambition that he has been secretly cherishing, which seem
to gain a wonderful encouragement from unexpected
events, which are deepened by some counsellor less
scrupulous than himself. And then come the oppor-
tunities for the crime. . . . Before it is done, the
Conscience which has been resisted within presents
itself in outward visible forms, the bloody dagger, the
handle towards the hand which cannot be clutched.
After it is done there rise before the imagination of
the man ghastly figures which recall those whom he
has put out of his way; the phantoms of superstition
must be laid by fresh acts which the former have made
desirable. The superstitions do not cease with the
dark deeds, they become more fixed, more intense. .
. . That is an ower true tale for the reign of Vic-
toria as well as for the reign of Elizabeth or of Duncan.

⁎

Do you know Lord Byron's *Manfred?* Have you
read that wonderful play of the Conscience? It has
none of the variety of *Macbeth*. Byron had not Shakespeare's power of making us see a number of different
men, each distinct in himself, each acting on the thought
and life of the others. The interest is concentrated in
the hero. . . . No one who reads it can believe it

to be a mere work of imagination. There is a burning
individual experience in every sentence. Count Manfred has come of an ancient line. His castle is in the
Alps. . . . He revels in the grand forms of Nature.
But they have become, like everything else, an oppression to him. There is on him the burden of a great
crime. He has power over spirits. They are ready to
do his bidding, to give him anything that he asks. He
asks forgetfulness. That is the one thing they cannot
give. . . . He is on the edge of a precipice. Why
may he not throw himself over it? What if he did?
Will the vision depart? A chamois hunter saves him
and brings him to his castle. At length the destined
hour arrives. A priest visits him in his dying hours,
a kindly well-intentioned man willing to use his knowledge and the powers of his office for the good of his
fellow-creature. It is in vain. What are subordinate
agents to him? He is face to face with the powers of
good and of evil. Which is the stronger? Which is
to prevail?

* *

The strictly domestic story has become characteristic
of our times, not in this country only, but . . . in
all countries of Europe. . . . The Family may be
merely a ground-plot for the display of sensational
incidents. Still these incidents are found to be most
startling and therefore most agreeable to those who

wish to be startled, when they are associated with out-
rages of one kind or another upon family order.
Those who do not want such stimulants to their own
feelings and fancies, and do not hold it an honest trade
to mix them for others, have found in the quietest
home-life materials for Art. All social harmonies and
social contradictions they see may come forth in the
relations of fathers and children, husbands and wives,
brothers and sisters, masters and servants. There is a
certain character, they are sure, which helps to make a
family peaceful or miserable — a home out of which
blessings or curses may diffuse themselves over the
commonwealth. . . . I am entitled therefore to
claim the authority of the most thoughtful, as well as
the most popular authors, of all schools, and of both
sexes, for the opinion that Domestic Morality is not
only an integral portion of Social Morality, but should
be the starting point of all discussions respecting it.

I do not think there is any kind of writing in our
day which is so popular as what is called "the Analysis of human feelings and motives." I am not speaking of philosophical books . . . I am thinking of
newspapers, magazines, novels. The greatest talent,
so far as I know, which is to be found in any of these,
is exhibited, not in the invention of plots, not in that

which is properly the dramatist's art, the showing forth
of persons in action, but in the careful dissection of
their acts, and of the influences which contributed to
the formation of their acts. . . . Though there is
much delicacy of observation in all the more eminent
Essayists of the last century, in the best of them a
calmness which I am afraid we have almost lost —
though a novelist like Fielding had a very remarkable
insight into many of the deceptions which men practise on themselves, as well as into some of their better
impulses — yet in the peculiar kind of observations
and criticisms to which I am referring, I doubt if they
could bear comparison with several of our contemporaries who in mere artistical gifts may be far inferior
to them. Criticism is that of which our age boasts,
and in which no doubt it excels. We are nothing, if
not critical.

(Fielding) was a Metropolitan Justice of the Peace;
he had known personally something of those who came
before him in that capacity, much also of the life of
ordinary citizens and country squires, of schoolmasters
and clergymen. In them, as well as in the servants
who waited upon them, and in the highwaymen who
were their terror, he discovered different exhibitions
of character, different standards of behavior, different

apprehensions of justice and injustice, of right and of wrong. In every class there was evidently *some* standard; in every one some apprehension of justice and injustice, of right and wrong. If these had been absent, the members of such classes could not have been represented in any story; they would not have been subjects for a work of Art. The novelist does not pretend to try them by any canons of his; but he makes us feel that they had their canons, and denounced acts which appeared to them a departure from their canons.

*

I used to feel a little irritated when I read Mr. Thackeray's novels by his frequent interpellations of " Well, Sir, or Well, Madam, do you treat your servants or your neighbors any better than these gentlemen or ladies whom I am describing, treated theirs?" The repetition seemed to savor of mannerism; the writer appeared to be excusing offences which deserved condemnation. I do not think so now. I believe Mr. Thackeray was aware of the temptation which there was in himself to forget the command, "Judge not that ye be not judged;" and felt that he should be doing his readers harm if he suffered them to forget it. He was trying honestly to correct a tendency which our age cherishes, and which the most deservedly popular talent may foster.

*
* *

We ought to look upon books not as a collection of written letters, but as the utterances of living men; if they are not, they are nothing. There may be much cruelty, often much baseness, in the exposures which are made of the ways and habits of authors who have not been in the least anxious to obtrude themselves upon the world, who have only wished to say something which they thought they had to say. But on the whole it is good that a man should be recognized as a being, and not merely as a speaker; as having spoken something out of his own very self. At all events, for good or for evil it has come to pass that our discourses of every kind tend to assume a personal character. Our statesmen, soldiers, preachers, must either be photographed, or sketched by an artist who thinks he understands their features better than the sun does. To complain of that which one finds so much the habit of our time as this is useless and not very wise. We are a part of our time; its ways are our ways: in finding fault with them, we are sure to be unconsciously finding fault with ourselves.

*
* *

The novels of Scott, lover of feudalism as he was, showed a genuine unpatronizing sympathy with human nature in its humblest forms, of which it can scarcely be said that there were any clear traces in our litera-

ture since the time of Shakespeare. Evidently the
doctrine of the illustrious plowman of his land, "a
man's a man for a' that," had taken possession of his
mind; courtly influences might weaken, but could not
expel it. There were no doubt fashionable novelists
who would gladly have restored the Chesterfield con-
ception of life, and who had admiring readers in the
middle class eager for what glimpses they could get
about the doings of the highest. Such ambition there
will always be in a country like ours, and writers willing, perhaps more or less able to gratify it. But on
the whole, the tendency has been in the other direction. Those who have helped us to understand the
forms of Society which are found under different conditions in all classes — of which we can in some measure judge for ourselves — have exercised the greatest
influence over us. Even a writer like Lord Byron,
possessed by the feelings of his own order, not much
honoring any other, was listened to, not chiefly on that
account, but because he showed that beneath the artificial surface of his circumstances and his character,
there lay springs of terrible passion which belong to
the kind, not the class.

I think a critical age wants to be reminded that it is
criticising itself; and critical men that they are criticising themselves. We are apt to forget that there is

a critic within us, a sterner, fairer judge than we are,
who is taking account of what we do and speak and
think; who is now and then saying to me when I am
pouring out any righteous indignation against the
robber of the ewe lamb, . . . " *Thou art the man.*"
The Casuist is called to remind us of this fact. He
must say to the critic, "Yes, this analysis of other
men's acts and motives is wonderfully clever and acute.
It may do those much good whom you desire to im-
prove. But then am not I, are not you — conscious of
something which is nearer than that man's acts and
motives? You pronounce what he ought to have
done, and not to have done. Is not that 'ought' and
'ought not' derived from a Conscience to which thou
canst appeal in him, because it is in thee?" . . .
When the critical temper is diffused through a land so
that it affects all classes, all ages, both sexes, when it
receives so much nourishment from all that we read,
and all that we hear, it does seem well that this branch
of our education should not be cast aside as if it had
lost its meaning. No general Philosophy can supply
the place of a personal Philosophy in an age which
loves Personality so much as ours loves it.

V.

ART.

ONE whole book of Plato's *Republic* is given to the subject of music as an instrument of education. He was but commenting on a pursuit which already formed a capital part of his country's discipline; and he felt that portion of it to be so important for good and for evil . . . that a careful criticism of the kinds of music which were likely to nerve and elevate, or to weaken and lower the character, was not out of place in a work written to teach Athenians, Greeks, and men, the principles on which they must live together, and the methods by which they might become practically united.

***

. . . Even the vulgarest street music is an education to the hearts of those who stand at the doors of pestilential dwellings to listen to it. Till that day which shall unseal all pent-up words and reveal the secrets of all hearts, it may not be known what thoughts have been stirred up in human spirits by

sounds which fell utterly dead upon our ears: what
authentic tidings came to them through those channels
when other avenues seemed to be closed; what awaken-
ings of conscience, what aspirations after truths, never
yet perceived, what search for treasures that had been
lost. Some of the most beautiful passages of modern
as of ancient poetry turn upon the stories of fishermen
and shepherds who were tempted by siren visions, that
spoke to them of some fairer regions, for which it
were well to desert the dreariness of their earthly
occupations, even at the risk of plunging into the
deep. . . . I feel that the beauty of such conceptions lies in their essential truth. The shepherds and
fishermen of our land, as of every land, hear these
whispers, have these dreams. They need an interpreter: if they do not find one, they may give heed
to any tempter who would lead them into the most
perilous depths, or the most wretched shallows. The
last calamity is the greater of the two. To have any
gratification for such longings is almost better than to
have them stifled and killed.

If Music thus becomes a common language, it must
have all the glory which those who have loved it best
and understood it most have felt to be in it. It must
be deeper than our ordinary speech. However, many
may be the different forms which it has put on among

different races, suitable to the tempers and habits of those races, it cannot be limited by these: it must be the sign that all are alike men : it must be the attempt —if as yet only an imperfect attempt—to express that which is human, that which binds us together.

I cannot disbelieve, though I may be utterly unable to comprehend it, anything which musicians have told us of the inner harmonies of which they have been made conscious. The beautiful sympathies, the clear pure lives of such men as Felix Mendelssohn, of such women as Mrs. Goldschmidt, should awaken in us much more than an admiration of them, though that may be most cordial. We should hail them as witnesses that those who have most of what is called musical acquirement, are those who most regard it as a bond to all their suffering brothers and sisters. We should assure ourselves that every divine gift to individuals is precious only as it unites them more with their kind.

. . . You must put yourself in the place . . . of some simple clown, all whose work has been of the roughest kind, but who has had a father and mother, perhaps a wife and children, and who possesses the strange power, which it has never occurred to him to think about, of recollecting that which has been in his own life, of anticipating that which shall be. . . . I cannot tell what these strange sounds, so unlike the ordinary discourse which he hears when he is talking about the weather, or buying and selling in the market, mean to him, what kind of message they carry to him: but I am quite sure it has something to do with these memories and hopes and fears of his; that it joins itself to a number of vague feelings which he has had about other days and about faces which he has seen, and hands which he has pressed; that it gives them a kind of distinctness which they had not before. . . . The music speaks to something within him which the ordinary language does not speak to, something more near his own very self, touching wires which that language does not reach, and making them vibrate.

⁂

I know nothing of pre-Raphaelite controversies. . . . But if any persons say that we ought to look straight at Nature, hoping that in due time she will reveal her meaning to us, if it is ever so slow in coming, and that, in the meantime, we are not to anticipate her lessons, or to put any of our notions or fancies into her by way of making her look prettier or more agreeable, this seems to me honest and true doctrine.

***

I am sure the right way to admire any great work of art is to know it thoroughly, to let it speak to you, and not to be in a hurry to form any opinion about it. What you say about the religion of the old Catholic pictures and the difficulty of receiving it in our days, has much truth in it. I used to mourn at the thought and to be pained by it. Now it gives me hope. I look upon Protestantism as unfriendly to Art, favorable to Science.

***

Science itself is becoming dynamical rather than mechanical: powers and agencies are discovered in nature itself, not less mysterious than those which miracle-workers spoke of. Man is able, through science, to exercise such powers as seem to attest the dominion of spirit over nature more completely than any signs they wrought. The victories of the old artist over the marble, the mysterious energy by which he compelled it to express the thoughts and emotions of living beings, are leading many whom these facts do not impress, in the same direction: the legends of Greece are received as striking commentaries on the powers of her sculptors and poets. The Romish priests, as teachers of youth, see that a movement is going on very like that which the popes rashly encouraged at the revival of letters. Some of them cry out

that it must be checked. . . . "Let us banish the
classics from our schools. The Greek legends are cor-
rupting our youth. They and profane art must be
proscribed." . . . Many in Protestant England .
. . would be ready to join them in their prohibitions.
There are those among us who think that the facts of
science, unless they are well sifted and sorted by religious men and mixed with religious maxims, are
likely to disturb the faith of the people, and that the
beautiful forms of Greek sculpture . . . must
corrupt their morals. . . . Our education in the
Bible ought to have taught us to believe in a God of
Truth — to reverence facts because they must be His
facts — to long that laws should be discovered because
they are His. . . . Our Bible culture ought to
have made us understand that nothing is impure save
the corrupt and darkened conscience and will. . . .
The breadth, simplicity, nakedness of the Scripture
language should have taught us to dread what is dis-
guised and dressed up for the purpose of concealment
as immoral and dangerous — to regard the study of
forms as they came from the Divine hand, with the
beauty which He has impressed upon them, as safe
and elevating.

* *

The exquisite instinct of Raphael perceived at once
the necessity of combining this event (the curing of

the epileptic boy) with the seemingly incongruous one of which we have just spoken (the Transfiguration). He felt that the unities of time and space were both to be sacrificed for the sake of the deeper and more mysterious unity which all three Evangelists had perceived, and which had compelled them to exhibit the earthly crowd and faithless disciples at the bottom of the mount, as part of the same picture with the still and awful scene upon its summit. The painter, if he transgressed the formal rules of his art, will be admitted, I should conceive, to have done so in submission to a higher principle of art: not for the sake of a broad and glaring contrast, but that he might give a reality to our feeling of the Transfiguration, that he might connect it with ourselves, he made his daring experiment. All laws of art rest, I suppose, on some ground deeper than themselves which they indicate, but cannot touch.

**

The genius of Raphael has brought the vision of Ezekiel home to the imaginations, if not to the hearts of a number of cultivated men in all parts of Europe, who would not have cared to study the Prophet himself. His picture is certainly worth a great many commentaries. And it has this especial merit: it justifies his own art from a charge which Protestants are often inclined, and not without much plausibility, to bring

against it. They complain that whenever it is applied
to the highest subject of all, it must of necessity lower
the idea of God, removing the thick cloud or the
brightness into which no eye can look, and presenting
some form which it is possible for us to apprehend and
conceive. That there is this peril in sacred painting
it would be folly to deny; that it may become the
tool of the senses, and of sensual worship, experience
has proved. . . . But the moral sense which is
exercised to discern good and evil, may be trusted to
pronounce a safe general verdict: the conscience of
each man may warn him to avoid that which does him
mischief. . . . The painter, I think, may be a
blessed help. . . . He may give us a total impression
of the Divine awfulness, of a glory that cannot be seen
or uttered, and yet make us feel that a Man is in the
midst of the throne, sustaining all things by the Word
of his power. The spirit which rests in this belief,
and is kept by it from sinking, will not be satisfied
with any outward image or picture. It will recognize
an unfathomable depth below; but a depth which we
can only see through and in the Man of Sorrows, an
abyss of love in which we can be content to be lost.

In reading a famous poem, or in studying a work
of art, it is far safer — it shows a far greater trust in
the author — to confess to ourselves what there is in
him, which we have not learnt to admire, than to affect

a vague and general worship because we suppose we ought to pay it. Sir Joshua Reynolds, in a noble passage of his Lectures, has enforced this duty upon his pupils, strengthening the exhortation by his own example. When he first looked upon an Italian masterwork, he had honesty to own to himself that he did not see how it had deserved its great name. He waited for light and it came to him. If divines exercised the same wisdom — grounded on the same fidelity to the verdict of the conscience, and the same trust that what is good will at last prove itself to be good — it is not to be told from how much uneasy scepticism respecting the facts and lessons of Scripture, from how much discontent, dangerous because suppressed, respecting the ordinances and creeds of the Church, they would save their disciples. Oftentimes they would see the very same change gradually taking place in them which our great painter describes in himself. That which seemed to them tame, cold, ungenial in the Bible story, — vague, or too definite and formal in the words of the old Confession, — would come forth in its simplicity and power; . . . would compel the admiration which they had refused to counterfeit, sweeping away what opposed its entrance.

**

The face of man we call, and rightly call, the human face divine. He who was the brightness of the

Father's glory had the face and features of a man. Painters have not been wrong in thinking that, though it was and must have been a face of sorrow, the sorrow, being the effect of intense sympathy, revealed the glory as nothing else could have revealed it.

* *

St. John is sometimes called the Apostle of Love. That they might give us that impression of him, painters have chosen to represent the last of the Apostles — who must have written all his books in his old age, perhaps in extreme old age — as a beardless youth with a delicate complexion and a feminine expression. I hope Mr. Ruskin has warned us . . . sufficiently of departures from fact, of false ideals, by whatsoever great names they may have been sanctioned. This mode of conceiving St. John, is especially misleading and mischievous. Hitherto in this Epistle he has spoken much of righteousness; only once about men loving each other, and that in connection with keeping a commandment; only once about God's love to us, and that in connection with our doing righteousness. His language has been simple and broad; not sentimental, at all. . . . His discourse . . . has been that of a man deeply experienced, not in the least of one whose countenance was not furrowed by thought and sorrow. It has been that of one who has known temptations and has been out in rough weather, not in the least of one, who has kept himself from contact with evil lest it should spoil his innocence.

* *

No great man really does his work by imposing his maxims on his disciples; he evokes their life. Correggio cries after gazing intently on a picture of Raphael, "I too am a painter," not one who will imitate the great Master, but who will work a way for himself. The teacher who is ever so poor in talent or information, but who is determined to speak out the convictions he has won, who is willing now and then to give some hint of the struggles through which he has won them, — leads one or another to say "I too am an *I*." The pupil may become much wiser than his instructor, he may not accept his conclusions, but he will own, " You awakened me to be myself, for that I thank you."

* *

Painting, it will be said, is born and cradled amidst softer airs and more genial influences (than poetry ;) that at least requires patronage and leisure to foster it. Let us hear what testimony there is on this subject. I need not refer to any other authority, since I cannot refer to a higher, than Mrs. Jameson's "Memoirs of the Early Italian Painters." After pointing out the mistake 'into which many historians have fallen in placing Cimabue at the head of the great revolution in art in the thirteenth and fourteenth centuries, Mrs. Jameson says that the great merit of that artist was in perceiving and protecting the talent of Giotto, "than whom no single human being of whom we read has exercised in any particular department of science or art a more immediate, wide and lasting influence." And then she tells a story which has often been told before, but never in clearer or more agreeable language than this: — "About the year 1289, when Cimabue was already old and at the height of his fame, as he was riding in the valley of Perpignano, about fourteen miles from Florence, his attention was attracted by a boy who was herding sheep, and who, while his flocks were feeding around, seemed intently drawing on a fragment of slate, with a bit of pointed stone, the figure of one of his sheep, as it was quietly grazing before him. Cimabue rode up to him, and looking with astonishment at the performance of the untutored boy, asked him if he would go with him and learn. To which the boy replied that he was right willing if his father were content. The father, a herdsman of the valley, by name Bondone, being consulted, gladly consented to the wish of the noble stranger, and Giotto henceforth became the inmate and pupil of Cimabue."

This story . . . goes much further, when it is connected with her remarks, than merely to prove, what no one perhaps, would have doubted, that a shepherd boy may become a great artist. It shows that the refinement and cultivation of a man like Cimabue, sprung from the upper classes of society, commanding all the appliances for his art which were within any man's reach in his time, and possessing himself the divine gift which could turn them to account, was not able to produce any deep and lasting impression upon the arts in Italy, till he had evoked the genius of this herdsman's son. . . . I have been more anxious to speak of these Florentines, because it is to Florence that the supporters of the doctrine, that leisure is the necessary and natural support of learning, commonly turn with the greatest confidence and satisfaction.

*

If Raphael fell, as we are told he did, below elder painters in his standard of devotion and holiness, I must think, without pretending to any knowledge of the subject, that he was not only more perfect than they were in his art, but that he did much more to raise the human and domestic affections, by exhibiting the purest model of them. I must think, also, that it was better and more for the honor of God, that men should study the human form as He made it, whether they derived the impulse to that study from the Greeks or from any other people, than that they should reconstruct it according to notions and fictions of their own. Any passage out of the artificial to the living and the real, must, I conceive, have been a passage towards moral health and reformation.

**

I do not know how many of you may have seen Mr. Holman Hunt's picture of the Awakened Conscience. Those who have seen it will not, I fancy, have forgotten it. . . . There are only two (figures) a man and a woman sitting in a somewhat gaudily furnished room beside a piano. His fingers are on the instrument. His face, which is reflected in a mirror, is handsome and vacant, evidently that of a man about town who supposes the brightest part of creation is intended to minister to his amusement. A music book on the floor is open at the words, " Oft in the stilly night." That tune has struck some chord in his companion's heart. Her face of horror says what no language could say, " That tune has told me of other days when I was not as I am now." The tune has done what the best rules that ever were devised could not do. It has brought a message from a father's house.

**

* Twenty-five years ago, if half a dozen intelligent people acquainted with the tendencies, the strength,

* Written in 1854.

the deficiencies of the English character, had been asked what studies would be . . . *least* likely to spread among us, especially among our manual workers, . . . they would have said one and all, "Whatever other instruction you give, leave the fine arts alone. They belong to the South. There they have ripened under the warm sunshine both of ecclesiastical and state patronage ; there men in the highest classes cultivate them, men in the lowest admire them. . . . Everything in the social condition of our people, in their hard practical temper, in their religious services, is hostile to this sort of cultivation." And if it occurred to any of the party, that possibly some unwashed Morland, or Blake or Gainsborough, might be dwelling in some unvisited corner of our land, a reluctant exception might perhaps have been made in favor of *Drawing*, only that the testimony might be more strong against the possibility of *Music* ever obtaining the slightest hold upon our people. How clearly it would have been explained to us, why voice and ear have been denied to the inhabitant of this island, and why, on the whole, we should rejoice in our freedom from the temptations to which they would expose us ! What a number of ingenious theories about races would have been introduced ! . . . And if these theories dwelt a little too strongly upon the effect of Italian sweetness and Roman Catholic worship, and so left the fact unexplained that Protestant Germany, with anything but a soft tongue, anything but a warm devotion, had nevertheless, given birth to eminent composers, and to a people musically inclined, I need not tell any one who knows from experience the elasticity of these philosophical explanations, how easily they would have expanded to take in this new and troublesome case — the speculative or mystical character of Germany always coming in as a resource, to prevent us from building any vain hopes upon our community of blood. Well, it has appeared in the result, that these clear and irresistible reasonings belong to the same class with the solutions which the members of the Royal Society, shortly after its foundation, sent in to the celebrated problem of Charles II. respecting the fish which did not displace the water. There was no problem to be solved; the fact so well accounted for was not a fact. Of all experiments in English education, beyond comparison the most successful has been that for diffusing a knowledge of music and a love of music among our people.

Music will never, surely, occupy a most conspicuous place in any good scheme of education. But if it has taken stronger hold of those whom we desire to educate, than any other study has done, especially if it has laid hold of them when we thought that any other study was more in agreement with their previous tastes and habits of mind, there must be something in it which may help us to understand what is needed in all studies, something which may deepen and widen our thoughts respecting the nature of education itself.

VI.

DUTY.

Our instruments, our hands, our hearts, are given us to work with in *this* time, to struggle with the evil, to bring out the good, in *this* time, in order that people may look back in after days, and say, " See what has come down to us from it; see what good has removed all the wrong which those who dwelt in it tell us of; see what there is in it to imitate."

***

How strongly I am convinced that we spend half our time in *thinking* of faith, hope and love, instead of in believing, hoping and loving! How utterly we forget that the very meaning of the words implies that we should forget ourselves, and themselves (the acts, I mean,) in the objects to which they refer.

***

You are sure to go wrong if you tie yourself by artificial rules, and ask whether this or that act falls within the letter of them, instead of considering what it is that we expect from others, and therefore what it is that we ought to give them.

⁕

I dream sometimes of times when one might have more inward and less outward business; but after forty years' experience I find that the inward is not better in my case, but worse for want of the outward, and that I really seek God most when I need His help to enable me to do what He has set me to do.

⁕

There is the lesson to us that each man has his appointed work to do, that more than that work he cannot do; that, if he does it as ever in his great Taskmaster's eye, the times to come may bless his memory and give thanks for his wisdom.

⁕

It seems to me that what we want is not a repudiation of service as inhuman, but a much profounder reverence for it: not an assertion that all have a right to rule, but far rather a conviction that every one is bound to serve, and may claim service as his highest privilege.

⁕

. . . Everyone of us is a servant or minister in this kingdom. Some of us have the name of Ministers. That is not that we may be separate from our fellows, but that we may give them a sign what Christ would have them be. All of us are ministers. Every father is a minister of Christ to his children.

Every mother is a minister of Christ to her children. . . . Wherever we are going, whatever we are doing, we are ministers of Christ. That is our calling. We may be faithful or unfaithful ministers; but He is our Master, and He has set us to wait upon some or other, upon more or fewer.

**

We have fallen into the notion that we shall work more energetically with our hands and with our brains because we are continually fretting ourselves about what will come of our work, what pence or praise we shall get by it. And yet every one of us knows in his heart that this fretting destroys the honesty of his work and the effects of his work. If we could be free from this perpetual fever, if we could work from an internal impulse, not under the pressure of external motives — if we could work as freemen, not as galley slaves — what a difference it would make to the health of our bodies and of our spirits, and to all our influence upon Society!

**

As Nature, with her old mosses and her new spring foliage, hides the ruins which man has made, and gives to the fallen tower and broken cloister, a beauty scarcely less than that which belonged to them in their prime, — so human love may be at work too, "softening and concealing and busy with her hand in healing" the rents which have been made in God's nobler temple, the habitation of His own spirit.

***

. . . What is it to serve the covetous god? It is this. If I am fretful and anxious about what I shall eat and drink, and how I shall be clothed, I fancy that I am his subject. I act as if he, this grudging, covetous god, were my master. And what is it to serve the Father in Heaven? If I work without fear or anxiety, believing that there is one over me who knows what I am doing, and takes an interest in it, and desires that my work should be healthy and profitable, then I am serving my Father in Heaven; then I am acting as if He were my Master.

***

Every act of mercy which our higher science is able to accomplish for sufferers from sickness, becomes a witness for God; so the work of every magistrate becomes a witness for Him equally: so commerce as it extends the bonds of fellowship between lands, and shows how one can give what another lacks, bears a witness no less mighty and effectual.

***

The harder a man works, the more he learns that he cannot let his thoughts go astray. They must be fixed somewhere. They must be turned to some one who will show him how he must pursue his business heartily, not lazily, honestly, and not like a rogue; as a freeman, not as a slave. Abide in this Lord of your hearts; set your heart upon Him, and you will get this help.

*
* *

I would have all laymen feel that they are called by God to their different offices, but I do not think they will feel it if we (clergymen) do not feel our call more distinctly, and assert it against all doubts in our own minds and apparent contradictions from without. We are called and we may believe that we are.

*
* *

. . . If (God) shows me any way in which I can lawfully give help, I think I shall not be slow to take it. . . . I hope it is not altogether cowardice, though I may have a great leaven of it, which makes me tremble to run where I am not sent or have no message. I know God is working; if I may work with Him, it is a blessing unspeakable; but to let His working by mine is terrible.

*
* *

Every one of you will be called to some position in which he will be both Servant and Master, in which he will be under Authority, in which he will have some under his authority. What your lives shall be, what good or mischief you will do to your country, — will depend mainly upon the question how you understand this position, what you suppose to be the nature

of this authority. Just so far as you forget that the
position involves a relation, just so far as you confound
the Authority with Dominion, your manners will become brutalized, just so far you will help to brutalize
all with whom in any capacity you are associated. .
. . By our fruits we shall be known and judged.
By our conduct to Servants it will be shown whether
we are fit to be Masters, or whether we must sink
into Servants of Servants.

**

The recollection of Liberty, the hope of Liberty,
may come to any, as Epictetus said, who find that
there is a stronger force within than the likings and
impressions which fasten themselves to outside things.
The Conscience is bidding each of us seek for that
liberty; we cannot be content till we have found it.

**

Let no one persuade you that the great teachers of
former ages must be cast aside in order that you may
profit by the wider experiences of your own day. If
you despise them, those wider experiences will be no
experiences for you; you will carry away a multitude
of notions from a multitude of schools; each will trip
up the other and make it useless for you. These
writers, if you use them rightly, will show you the
worthlessness of mere notions, the impossibility of
separating Morality from Life. Mr. Buckle repeats

the words, "As you would that men should do unto you, do ye also to them likewise," and asks triumphantly what they have effected for mankind? Speaking according to the lessons of the book in which they occur, I should answer, "Nothing whatever if they are regarded as mere words in a book; worse than nothing if they are taken as warrants for self-exaltation, as reasons for exalting ourselves as Christians above other men."

. . . I have sometimes thought I might be of use in warning those for whom I feel a deep and strong interest against a tendency which I feel in myself, and which I have seen producing most melancholy effects. I mean a tendency to be quick-sighted in detecting all errors in the schemes of other men and to set up their own in opposition to them.

Only let us each work in the calling whereto God has called us, and ask Him to teach us what it is, and we shall understand one another and work together.

I have a very strong feeling of the duty of testifying for the name and kingdom of God; a very deep conviction that Protestants and Romanists alike are setting up a religion in place of God. . . . I feel

that if ever I do the work which I am sent into the
work to do, I must more earnestly call upon the Church
to believe in God, the Father, the Son, and the Spirit.

**

We may appeal to men by the terrors of a future
state; we may use all the machinery of revivalists to
awaken them to a concern for their souls: we may
produce in that way a class of religious men who pursue an object which other men do not pursue (scarcely
a less selfish, often not a less outward object) — who
leave the world to take its own course, who, when
they mingle in it, as in time they must do for the sake
of business and gain, adopt again its maxims, and become less righteous than other men in common affairs,
because they consider religion too fine a thing to be
brought from the clouds to the earth. . . . But
we must speak again the ancient language that God
has made a covenant with the nation, and that all citizens are subjects of an unseen and righteous King, if
we would have a hearty, inward repentance, which will
really bring us back to God: . . . which will go
down to the roots of our life, changing it from a self-
seeking life to a life of humility and love and cheerful
obedience; which will bear fruit upwards, giving no-
bleness to our policy and literature and art, to the
daily routine of what we shall no more dare to call
our *secular* existence.

* *

"What shall we have therefore?" was the thought of the Apostle, as well as of the ruler. "Everything," is the answer, "gifts beyond your imagination; but this is the greatest: To understand that your calling and your work are themselves inconceivable blessings, and that *the* blessing which follows upon them, the hire at the end of the day, is one of which you are not to be possessors, but sharers. If you look upon it as something which you are to 'have,' and from which others are to be excluded for your sake, you will never know what it is." . . . To be like Him, to enter into His mind, is *the* good: this is what the chosen seek: those who fancy themselves chosen to the injury of their brethren are only called. What a lesson to the elect nation! What a deeper, more awful lesson to the elect Church!

* *

As it was Christ in Paul who was suffering and striving for the Church — the object of his instruction, of his suffering, of his Gospel, was to make each Gentile, each man, know that Christ was in him, the very Christ who was in his brother: therefore, that he was not to exalt himself above his brother, was not to dream of high mystical flights and raptures, by which he might scale heaven, but in toiling, suffering, teaching, was to enter into the loving mind of his Lord.

* *
*

We have seen that sacrifice infers more than the giving up of a *thing*. We shall have to ask how the *person* who presents it may be enabled to give up himself, and into what errors he may fall in his effort to do so. We have seen that sacrifice has something to do with sin, something to do with thanksgiving. . .

. We have seen that sacrifice is offered by man, and yet that the sacrifice becomes evil and unmoral, when the man attaches any value to his own act, and does not attribute the whole worth of it to God. It will be our duty to ask, how it is possible that man should present the sacrifice, of which God is at once the Author and the Acceptor.

* *
*

The Kingdom of God begins within, but it is to make itself manifest without. It is to penetrate the feelings, habits, thoughts, words, acts, of him who is the subject of it. At last, it is to penetrate our whole social existence, to mould all things according to its laws.

* *
*

Is it easy to do the commonest acts, . . . as if they were not our own, as if we were to carry out in them the mind and will of another? Is it easy to know how these common acts ought to be done, so that they shall bring blessings and not misery, light

and not darkness, to our fellow-men ? If we are honest, we shall not talk so proudly and contemptuously
about *mere* duties and the great principle of faith.

* *

 . . . We may be very slow in listening to calls
of duty, and the reason may be that we regard Him
who calls us as an Exactor, not a Giver. I press this
confession before all others . . .   because I believe
we, the ministers of God, are more bound to make it
than other men. We have thought, it seems to me,
that our chief business was to persuade and conjure
and argue and frighten men into a notion and feeling
of their responsibilities; whereas our chief business is,
assuredly, to proclaim the name of God; to set that
before our fellow-creatures in its fulness and reality;
so to convince them of their sin ; *so* to teach them
how they may be delivered from it. . . .   We have
not dared to speak of God broadly, simply, absolutely,
as a Giver, lest we should thereby weaken His claim
upon man's obedience ; whereas this is His claim upon
their obedience. . . .   Thus we have begotten in
men a feeling that they are obliged to do something
which they cannot do. . . .   If we dared to look
upon God as a Giver in the full, free, intelligible sense
of the words, we should, in asking for bread, feel that
we were asking for the power and energy wherewith
to work for it.

* *

Your business is to trust the risen Lord with your secret hearts; to be believing in His perfect righteousness, and by faith to be clothing yourselves with His nature. Your business is to be fighting, as your forefathers fought, against all the temptations to distrust, cowardice, baseness, which are besetting you on every side. . . . By simplest acts of daily obedience, by continual efforts to be true, to speak truth, to follow truth, you are to prove that Christ's word is speaking to you, speaking in you: you are to show forth His risen life.

* *

Till we understand that there is something *due* from us, till the sense of *duty* is awakened, we have no freedom, we are not even in the way to become men.

* *

We are to be, as John the Baptist was, preachers of Repentance. We are to preach, like him, of a Baptism for the Remission of Sins. We are to preach, like him, of a coming day of the Lord. And all this the least of us may do, as he could not do it, provided we remember what Baptism we and our hearers have received; provided we have some slight, some growing impression of the Name into which we are baptized. That remembrance and that impression must make us feel as John the Baptist felt — that the position of

men brought into covenant and communion with God
is a grand one, involving great responsibilities. Like
him, we must exhort men to confess — we must confess — how little we have remembered, how ill we have
acquitted ourselves of, those responsibilities. In en-
couraging our hearers, one and all, to this confession,
we may know, as surely as John did, that we are
speaking as God would have us speak, — that we are
speaking His words, not ours. . . . But we shall
know also, what John could know very imperfectly,
that every call to Repentance is a message from a
Father, coming down to us through a Son, made effectual for us by a Spirit.

***

What danger that the well-being of hundreds of millions may be less dear to us than the triumph of a
party, — nay, that we may make grand sentences about
the hundreds of millions into mere tools for working
out our own beggarly and selfish triumphs! What
probability that, not grand philanthropy only, but private friendship, once most cordial, — love, once passionate and deep — may become chilled . . . by
petty jealousies and suspicions. And yet more perilous still are those warm religious emotions which seem
to carry the very pledge and seal of eternity in them.
. . . How many arts will a man be tempted to use
that he may persuade himself they are not changed!

. . . How at last he may cast aside all faith, de-
claring that he knows it to be a delusion, and that he
would save others, if he could from the imposture to
which he has yielded! Where was his original mistake? What is the original falsehood of all who speak
of their love to God and man? This: they take
credit to themselves for a love which is moving them
to noble thoughts and good deeds, but which has
another source than their hearts; which is divine, not
earthly: universal, not partial. How may they be
saved from casting off all that is true in them, when
they discover that they have been false? By frankly
confessing that falsehood to the Spirit of Truth who
is convincing them of it.

***

. . . A very awful obligation is laid upon us by
the claims and boasts which we put forward to be
specially tolerant and merciful and charitable. I say
that to make such pretensions and not to fulfil them,
or only to fulfil them by a lazy indulgence which per-
mits any kind of wrong in others, which stirs up no
life or energy in us, is to place ourselves far below the
cruelest fanatics who had in them some zeal for human
beings as well as for God, however it might be per-
verted by their selfishness and pride. But I say also
that God would not allow us even to dream of such
an honor for ourselves as the use of these titles and of

these boasts (as Christians) implies, if He did not wish
us to have the dream turned into a reality. We may
have more charity, a deeper charity than we have
aspired to when our aspirations have been the grandest. For we may abandon the thought of having a
charity or love of our own, and so may be perfected
in love. We may yield ourselves to that love which
passes knowledge, that love which is a consuming fire
to destroy the grovelling petty desires, the party spirit,
the self-seeking that have made us a world of sects,
instead of a Church of brothers.

* * *

If we do not hate that which is contrary to love —
that which is contrary to the nature of God — we cannot truly and earnestly love. . . . I know that
there is always a danger of the hatred which we ought
to cherish in our heart of hearts against everything
which is cowardly, base, insincere, unlovely, passing
into that hatred of *men* which is a breach of the commandment; yes, the danger often seems to be greatest
in the strongest, most earnest minds. . . . No
doubt this was a temptation of reformers in other
days. They launched forth their denunciations against
men, some of whom we cannot help regarding with
respect and affection. . . . God give us their
zeal, for their *zeal* was all good and loving! God
teach us not to judge their fierce words, though we

may not imitate them, though we may sometimes lament them! For we should ask ourselves very seriously whether our calm, measured, demure phrases may not conceal more scorn that is meant to wound the heart of the man we are censuring . . . than those which we call them bigots and savages for uttering; just because we do not loathe the essential evil as they did, because we do not care so much for the essential good. This self-inquiry is, as I have hinted already, the true way to a distinction between a hatred of principles and a hatred of persons. To see the evil, first of all, in our own acts, in our own selves; to recognize it as marring our sincerity and worth —as degrading us from the level God intends for us— this is a security which we can obtain in no other way for our loving the man whose wrong doings we hate.

***

It is a comfort, an infinite comfort, to think that no divine word which goes out of our lips, is dependent for its truth, or even for its success, upon the purity of the lips, upon the right will or heart of the speaker. It is a comfort beyond all comfort to believe that *the* Will, *the* Heart, from which the good news has first proceeded, are without variableness, or the least shadow of turning. It is a comfort, in this sense, to feel that we are officials, open to the same charges and just charges of coldness and deadness as all others who

bear that name. But may we not ask of those who
hear as the one greatest sign . . . of the thankfulness to God for anything that has entered into them
and borne fruit, that they will desire this blessing for
their teachers, that they may be good stewards of the
manifold gifts of God: stewards, I mean, who have
not merely a dispensation committed to them, but who
respond to the mind and will of Him who has committed it, whose spirits are quickened and actuated
continually by His Spirit? Then I think, we — ceasing to be mere officials, and yet more than ever feeling
that there can be nothing more blessed and glorious
than duty, because He who exacts duty is Himself the
source of all loving sympathy and affection, . . .
shall be better able to help all classes and conditions
of men.

*
* *

The sense of duty draws all its strength and nourishment from the acknowledgment of a God who never
acts from caprice or self-will, who governs all things
in heaven and earth according to the order which He
has imposed upon them, who seeks to bring all voluntary beings into an understanding of His order and
into cheerful consent with it. Obedience and freedom
embrace each other when we believe that He asks us
to yield up our wills as sacrifices to His who has first
made the great sacrifice for us, who in that sacrifice

has united us to Himself. Then no office can be looked upon as anything less than a calling: in the highest and in the lowest Christ's own voice is saying, " Follow me."

***

Any Christian man who takes his stand upon the same ground of unity in the Church whereof Christ is the Head, who acts consistently with that position, fulfilling the office to which he is called, and not seeking some other to please himself, may become a witness in every land to which he goes of the fellowship into which his baptism has brought him ; may in his words or life expound the principle of this fellowship ; may show how universal its privileges are, and how each may for himself partake of them. But I know there must be many on whom the often-repeated words, " There are heathens at our doors, we ourselves are half heathens ; leave Buddhists and Mahometans till you have provided for these," will have an effect sufficient to destroy their interest in all such exhortations. . . . A faith which boasts to be for humanity cannot test its strength unless it is content to deal with men in all possible conditions. If it limits itself to England, it will adapt itself to the habits and fashions and prejudices of England, of England, too, in a particular age. But doing this, it will never reach the hearts of Englishmen. You say, " Try your Chris-

tianity upon the cotton-spinners of Manchester, upon
the hardware men of Birmingham; if it fail with
them, do you expect it will succeed in Persia and
Thibet?" We know it will fail, it must fail, in Birmingham and Manchester, if it addresses the people in
those places merely as spinners and workers in hardware. This has been the mistake we have continually
made. We have looked upon these "hands" as created to work for us; we have asked for a religion
which should keep the "hands" in the state in which
they will do most work and give the least trouble.
But it is found that they are men who use these hands;
and that which is a religion for hands is not one for
men. Therefore it becomes more evident every day
that there is a demand in Manchester and Birmingham
for that which, till we understand human beings better,
we cannot supply. To acquire that understanding, we
need not grudge a journey to Persia or Thibet; we
need not think it an idle task to inquire what people
want who are not called to spin cotton, or work in
hardware, but who are creatures of the same kind
with those who do.

***

Buddhism, then, like Hindooism and Mahometanism,
has its lesson for us. We are debtors to all these in a
double sense. Nor, I think, is it otherwise with those
modern infidels whose objections I have been consider-

ing. . . . Our obligations to them are not slight
if they have been sent to break down a low grovelling
notion we had formed of our own position and work.
. . . We owe them the deepest gratitude if they
have led us to ask ourselves whether there is any faith,
and what kind of faith it is, which must belong, not
to races or nations, but to mankind; still more, if
they have forced us to the conclusion that the real
test, whether there be such a faith, and whether it has
been made known to us, must be action, not argument;
that if it exist, it must show that it exists.

* *

That word "Conscience" is one on which we cannot
meditate too earnestly. You should consider it along
with the adjective "*conscious.*" You should consider
what you mean when you say "I am conscious" of
something. You should remember that it is derived
from two words signifying "to know," and "together
with." You must see that it implies that you know or
take account of something which is passing within
your own self. It leads us into this deeply solemn
thought that a man can not only perceive the things
that are without him, but that he has eyes within and
that there is a whole world for him there to contemplate. But this is an appalling reflection if we do not
pursue the thought higher, if we do not ascend from
the word "consciousness" to the word "Conscience,"

if we do not reflect that it is not our own voice merely that is speaking within, but the voice of another, the perfect Teacher, Reprover, Guide; and, if we do not believe that it is possible to ascend from the conscience of His presence into communion with His character and will.

**

" What would become of us," it has been asked, " if each *soldier* felt himself to be an I ; said for himself, 'I ought and I ought not?' My answer is this, I know not what would have become of us in any great crisis if this personal feeling had *not* been awakened; if every man had not felt that he was expected to do his duty; if duty had been understood by each sailor or soldier . . . as the dread of punishment; if the captain who asked for obedience had been just the person towards whom that slavish dread was most directed. Unless the obedience of our sailors and soldiers had been diametrically the reverse of that sentiment . . . I believe there is not a regiment which would not have turned its back in the day of battle, not a ship which would not have struck its flag. The charm of the captain's eye and voice, of his example and his sympathy, this, as all witnesses whose testimony is worth anything have declared, has had an electrical influence upon hosts which could enable them to face punishments from enemies considerably

more terrible than any which the most savage vengeance could devise for desertion.   It is not the thought
of what a majority will say or do that can stir any
individual man to stand where he is put and die.   It
is that he has been aroused to the conviction, " I am
here, and here I ought to be."

***

. . .   The Scripture . . .   represents all intellectual gifts as bestowed, not to raise one man above
another, but simply that men may be enabled to serve
each other.   The highest of all is the servant of all.
He who holds his gifts under this condition, and confesses his unfitness for the use of them, is a fellow-
worker with the Divine Spirit.   He is doing that which
he is sent here to do.

***

Change . . .   the long word Obligation into the
shorter homelier word Duty. . . .   The mother
tongue is always sweeter, often more distinct and definite, than the tongue of philosophers.   Happily when
we speak of persons, we cannot forget the affections
which we have for them. . . .   But there is a danger of treating those affections as if they created the
Order which calls for them.   If we fall into that mistake, the affections will become merely a part of our
pleasures or pains.   As long as we like a person, we
shall suppose we are bound to him ; our dislike will

dissolve the tie. We shall live in a circle of what are called in the cant of our day *elective affinities;* the grand old name of Relations will be treated as obsolete. That you may escape this danger, I dwell upon this fact that we are in an Order; that relations abide whether we are faithful to them or neglect them; and that the Conscience in each of us affirms "I am in this order, I ought to act consistently with it, let my fancies say what they please." . . . The reverence for parents, the sanctity of the marriage vow, the permanence of friendships, are all in peril from the confusion between likings and affections. Those who resolutely draw a distinction between them will have their reward. They will find that the Conscience protests not against the fervency, but against the coldness, feebleness, uncertainty of our affections.

*_**

Nothing that I know is more touching than Marcus Aurelius Antoninus' enumeration of the debts which he owed to his mother, to his predecessor who had adopted him, to his instructors in every department, to the friends who had preserved him from any flattery, who had given him hints for the fulfilment of any duty. For Duty meant to him exactly the reverse of that which it means in the philosophy of Mr. Bain. It was literally that which, under no dread of punishment, but with great thankfulness, he confessed to be *due* from him. He was aware of the temptation to neglect it; that was the slavish impulse; freedom to perform it was what he sought with all earnestness. . . . Philosophy was never an excuse to him for avoiding troublesome business. . . . He had a conscience of the bondage into which we bring ourselves by the neglect of little things: he would have accepted those grand words of our poet in his ode to Duty, which recognizes all freedom and all joy as springing from submission to its commands.

* *

Every one has some work to do. Every one has inducements to forsake that work for things which, whether pleasant to others or not, are pleasant to him. . . . Mr. Bentham's assumption that what is pleasant is natural, that Nature has appointed it for us, commends itself to his judgment. Only there is something in him which says, "I ought not. The agreeable thing will hinder me from doing the thing which I am occupied with. The agreeable thing accepted to-day will make me weaker to-morrow, less capable of determining my course, more the victim of the impulses and impressions that come to me from without."

* *

No doubt each step as we advance does make us more aware of that which we have to lift; (we learn) that the heaviest weight which a man has to bear is

himself. That is surely a hard lesson if there comes
with it no promise of a way in which he may throw
off himself. He has had hints upon that subject in
his previous experience. Each family relation has said
to him something about the possibility of losing himself in another; has taught him that he only realizes a
blessing when he confers it. This remembrance is not
enough for his present growth; his personal distinctness has been discovered to him; he cannot merely
fall back upon domestic sympathies. But they may
remain to illuminate the new road which he has entered; there may still be a way by which he can lose
himself and so find himself.

* *

The habit of measuring ourselves by others is one
into which we slide most easily, and which involves
continual unfairness to them, still greater to ourselves.
I ask why I may not indulge in extravagances in which
a man of twice or thrice my means indulges freely;
why I may not eat and drink what a man with twice
or thrice my strength or my labor perhaps needs. I
cling therefore to the "*I* ought" and the "*I* ought
not;" that will not interfere with the discovery and
acknowledgment of laws by which we are all bound;
it will prevent me from assuming the practice of this
man or that as the standard of mine, or my practice
as the standard of his.

***

Vainly, therefore, are we told that if there is a Conscience in each man that Conscience must be its own standard, that the only escape is to suppose a Conscience created by a Social Opinion. All such propositions look very plausible upon paper; bring them to the test of living experience and they melt away. There is that in me which asks for the Right, for that which ought to have dominion over me; there is that in me which says emphatically, "This is not that Right, this ought not to have dominion over me." I may be long in learning what the Right is; I may make a thousand confused efforts to grasp it; I may try to make it for myself; I may let others make it for me. But always there will be a witness in me that what I have made, or any one has made, is not what I ought to serve; that is not the right, not what I am seeking for, not what is seeking me.

***

Mr. Thackeray used to talk of week-day preachers and to demand a place among them for himself. As a Sunday preacher, I am inwardly and painfully convinced that no persons more require the kind of monition which he supplied than those whose regular business obliges them to tell other men of their wrong-doings and temptations. Their function cannot, therefore, I apprehend, supersede that of the Casuist.

Clergymen may learn from him, when they are preparing for their after work, some of the perils to
which it will expose them.

***

The Kingdom of Heaven is to me the great practical existing reality which is to renew the earth and
make it a habitation for blessed spirits instead of for
demons. To preach the Gospel of that Kingdom, the
fact that it is among us, and is not to be set up at all,
is my calling and business. . . . If ever I do any
good work and earn any of the hatred which the godly
in Christ Jesus receive, and have a right to, it must
be in the way I have indicated, by proclaiming society
and humanity to be divine realities *as they stand*, not
as they may become, and by calling upon the priests,
kings, prophets of the world to answer for their sin,
in having made them unreal by separating them from
that living and eternal God who has established them
in Christ for His glory.

VII.

ASPIRATION.

Every prayer is a renunciation of independence. *Every* prayer says "We can do nothing without Thee." As Christ's prayers were the essentially true prayers, they must have had this meaning perfectly, without any reservation.

***

Christ is in you; submit yourself to Him. Say, "Lord, I submit." Not now, but at every moment of your life: tell Him of whatever sins and sorrows are disturbing you: of *sins* no less than *sorrows;* of *sorrows*, no less than *sins.* . . . Ask that He will do His will in you, which is your blessedness.

***

We want a home for our hearts just as much as we want a home for our limbs. Every one of us is looking for such a home. We need something, as we say, to set our hearts upon, and we try a number of things. . . . We try various pleasures, some good, some bad, but none last long enough, none will give a man space to rest in, and those which suit one do not suit

another. And some desire to have some possession
which they cannot enjoy together, so they have to
struggle each one to drive out the other. Could there
not be a home for all? Could there not be something
in which we might abide for ever? There is such a
home for all. The home is a person, is a friend. We
are baptized into Jesus Christ: we put on His name;
we claim Him as the Lord and Friend and Brother of
us all. . . . "And now," says St. John, "act as if
this were so: act as if you had this Friend; let your
hearts stay in this home: do not go out of it."

**

The more sincerely and faithfully we deal with our
own minds, the more I believe we shall discover that
the highest knowledge of all does not come at once;
and *never* comes in phrases and abstractions. If man
is capable of knowing God, it must be because there
is that in him, that in every part of his being, which
responds to something in God.

**

Let each for himself long and pray that the evil
spirits which have had dominion over him may be cast
out now. Let us ask that we may become exorcists
ourselves. For is not every true and living man and
woman an exorcist? Is not every one who will yield
himself to be Christ's servant, permitted to deliver his
brother from some spirit which has enslaved him?

***

The formula that "our wishes are fore-feelings of
our capabilities" is, I believe, one of much beauty and
worth: . . . In looking back to the castles of ear-
liest boyhood, we may see that they were not wholly
built of air — that part of the materials of which they
were composed were derived from a deep quarry in
ourselves — that in the form of their architecture were
shadowed out the tendencies, the professions, the
schemes, of after years. Many may smile sadly when
they think how little the achievements of the man
have corresponded to the expectations of the child or
of the youth. But they cannot help feeling that those
expectations had a certain appropriateness to their
characters and their powers; that they might have
been fulfilled, not according to the original design, but
in some better way. I do not think that such retro-
spects can be without interest, or need be without
profit, to any one.

***

In desponding moods one may dream that a worship
based upon our own conceptions and likings — a worship which, because we invent it for ourselves, will
represent our lowest thoughts and confirm and deepen
those in us — may conquer all that has struggled with
it, all that has borne witness to us of a Life which is
higher than our own. But, when we are in our right

minds we know that this cannot be. The more stead-
fastly and earnestly we labor . . . for the progress
of Humanity . . . the more will the Worship to
which domestic Relations have led the way — the
Worship which seeks for a ground of Humanity beneath itself — expel the superstitions into which vulgar
men and philosophers equally are betrayed when they
make gods of their own and bow down before them.

***

I am a very bad proselytiser. If I could persuade
all dissenters to become members of my church to-
morrow, I should be very sorry to do it: I believe the
chances are that they might leave it the next day. I
do not wish to make them think as I think. But I
want that they and I should be what we pretend to
be, and then I doubt not we should find that there is
a common ground for all far beneath our thinkings.
For truth I hold not to be that which every man trow-
eth, but to be that which lies at the bottom of all
men's trowings, that in which those trowings have
their only meeting-point.

***

. . . We can come boldly to Him every day to
ask Him to make us true when we feel false, and brave
when we feel cowardly, and strong to act when we
feel as if we could do nothing. So this is a lesson for
us who are going about the world, as much as for

those who are on sick beds. We want healing — continual healing — just as they do. We want strength as much as they do: strength to be right and to do right: strength for the work that we have to do each day.

* *

May Christ give us honesty and courage to confess our blindness, that we may turn to Him who can make us see! May He deliver us from all conceit of our own illumination, lest we should become hopelessly dark!

* *

A man who feels that he is called to a work, does not, therefore, feel power to accomplish it. He may feel . . . an increased feebleness: but he understands that he may ask the Father, whose will he is called to do, that that will may be done: so he wins a strength which is and is not his own.

* *

Christ's prayer was the acknowledgment of that which had been revealed to Him, His filial acceptance of what had been prepared for Him. And surely, all prayer must be this. It is the acknowledging of that, be it sad or joyful, which has been given to us; it is the casting of our experience upon Him who has brought us into it and who understands it, because without Him we cannot go through it, or in the least understand it ourselves.

Christ can only say " *Father, save me from this hour,*" and yet He adds, " *For this cause came I unto this hour.*" It is not often that these actual signs of the struggle within Him are declared to us. How wise and necessary that we should have only rare and occasional discoveries of it! But of what unspeakable worth have these discoveries been to the hearts of sufferers in every age! The agony must be passed through; the death-struggle, which is most tremendous after the vision of coming good has been the brightest. But the sting of solitude, which is the sharpest of all, is taken out of it. Christ has cried " *Save me from this hour !* "

Do not attempt to analyze your feelings. Do not try to find out how much of them is excusable, how much not. God gives repentance, we do not make it. We may tell Him as well as we can what a mess and labyrinth we are in. We may at least say, "Guide us through it and out of it."

Hope for ourselves; hope for all; but hope of life, not of Death, of a real Heaven, not of a Heaven which is a pleasant Hell; this is what we want; this the spirit of God would keep alive within us.

A Church ought . . . to teach us in our public worship what a number of persons we have to do with in the common intercourse of life, and how solemn our relation to them all is, how certainly it has its ground in our common relation to God and is only understood and acted on when we refer it to Him. The suffrages which follow the Creed and Lord's Prayer have, as I conceive, the object, and might have the blessed effect of suggesting to Ministers and People what wishes they should be cherishing for each other and for all men; what should be the habits of their minds, whether they are speaking or silent; what kind of aspirations the Heavenly Father, who knows their necessities before they ask, would be drawing forth from them.

If, in spite of all reluctance, we determine not to go out in search of Christ into the deserts, not to shut ourselves in the secret chambers that we may have Him to ourselves there; if we will expect Him among the knaves and blackguards, and hypocrites of the world, and will act as if we believed they had the same right in Him that we have, . . . we shall be acquiring by degrees the power of recognition, the human sympathies which He is seeking to cultivate in us; we shall be winning a victory over the vanity and conceit which shut us up in our own little circles and lesser selves; we shall be preparing for the gathering together of all in Christ.

*
* *

The longing for personal sympathy has something right in it, but I suppose it is akin to disease, and whenever I am able to reflect wisely and earnestly, I desire that those who have ever got any good out of me, should grow much too old and wise for my teaching, and should not feel themselves cramped and chained by it. I had some terrible experiences many years ago from not learning that lesson, and wishing (secretly) that a dear friend who once regarded me as a sort of guide, should go on doing so, when he was fitter to guide me. Ever since his death, I have mourned over that vanity, and desired that I should never fall into it again.

*
* *

Every one of us may ask that Divine Word, who is near to us, and with us, for an understanding heart. Every one of us who feels that a great work is laid upon him . . . and that he is but a little child, may crave for a spirit to discern the good and the evil in himself and in all others. And if we feel . . . that what we need above all things else is that sense

of responsibility, that consciousness of a calling, that
feeling of feebleness, which were the source of Solomon's prayer, let us ask for these gifts first.

* *

It is possible to show that we love the truth more
than our opinions and ourselves, if we do love it more.
And there will be the rich reward of teaching others
to love it more than themselves and their opinions, and
so of making them in very deed our fellow-citizens
and fellow-workers.

* *

Oh, do not let the sluggish, turbid current of your
ordinary days seem to you that which truly represents
to you what you are, what you are able to be! No,
the time when you made the holiest resolutions, when
you struggled most with the powers of evil, when you
said it should not be your master, when Love con-
quered you and freed you from other chains that you
might wear her chains, *that,* that was the true index
to the Divine purpose concerning you: that tells you
what the Spirit of God is every hour working in you
that you may be. You may not be able to revive the
feeling which you had then, but He who gave you that
feeling, He is with you, is striving with you, that you
may will and do of His good pleasure. Only do not
strive with Him that He may leave you to yourself
and to the power of evil.

**

There must be a day when all things in heaven and earth which consist only by Christ shall be gathered manifestly together in Him, when it shall be known and confessed that there is one king, one priest, one sacrifice; that we have been at war with each other, because we have not done homage to that one king. .

. . And those who are willing before God's altar to own that their self-seeking and self-will have been rending asunder their families, the nation, the Church, the world, may hope that God's spirit will work in them henceforth to do all such acts as shall not retard, but hasten forward, the blessed consummation for which they look. They may ask to be taught the mystery of daily self-sacrifice — how to give up their own tastes, opinions, wishes. They may ask that they may never be tempted to give up one atom of God's truth, or to dally for one moment with the falsehoods of themselves or of their brethren : because truth is the one ground of universal peace and brotherhood, because falsehood and division are ever increasing and reproducing each other.

**

. . . The eagerness of our entreaty (that God's will may be done, God's kingdom may come) will depend, first, upon our belief that His is a good will and a good kingdom ; secondly, upon our experi-

ence that there is a very bad will and a very bad kingdom actually and perpetually resisting it; thirdly,
upon our confidence that we are meant to be fellow-
workers with our Father in heaven — meant, with the
energies of our wills, and the energies of our acts, to
assist in the victory of the true over the false.

"O Thou who knowest what I am, and where I
am, bring me out of these mists, these false, confused
lights, into the open day." A reasonable prayer if
God is merciful, and man is weak — if God is our
Father, and we are His children; the only prayer
oftentimes which it is possible for man to offer. . .
. He brings nothing; he casts himself in mere dependence and despair before One who must raise him,
if he is not to sink further and further; who must
make him true, if he is not to become falser and falser.

All heathen prayer supposes that a man knows his
own wants, and that He whom he worships may attend
to him when he makes them known with sufficient
clearness and earnestness. Its strength, therefore, lies
in much speaking. A number of arrows must be shot
at different distant marks that there may be a chance
of some hitting. All Christian prayer supposes that
our Father knows what we have need of before we

ask Him; that He makes us conscious of our needs, and leads us to declare them to Him. . . . But the words "Heathen" and "Christian" may be easily abused to purposes of self-exaltation and self-delusion. Our Lord never taught His disciples that they would be exempt from any of the temptations or evil inclinations of other men. Neither the Old Covenant nor the New, Circumcision or Baptism, Law or Gospel, Nation or Church, has the power to make us *in ourselves* a race of pure holy beings.

*_**

We know — we positively know — what the Cain offering is, because we have presented the like ourselves. We have prayed; and then have complained, just as the Jews did, that it has been all in vain, that no good has come of it. We have made sacrifices and we have wondered that we got no reward for them. Perhaps we have been angry that, being so good, we have not been more favored by fortune and circumstances. Perhaps we have been angry that, trying so hard to make ourselves good, we have succeeded so little. Perhaps we have had a general notion that God could not be persuaded to be gracious to us and forgive us, in spite of all the sacrifices we have offered, and that we must try others which are more costly. . . . Assuredly, this is the Cain spirit in us all. . . . Was not our sin that we *supposed* God to be an arbitrary Being whom we, by our sacrifices and prayers, were to conciliate? Was not this *the* false notion which lay at the root of all our discontent, of all the evil thoughts and acts which sprung out of it? We did not begin with trust, but with distrust; we did not worship God because we believed in Him, but because we dreaded Him.

If you study the construction (of the Collects) you will find that the principle "Our Father knoweth what things we have need of before we ask" is assumed in all of them. Some strong satisfying view of the character of God, of His love to men, of what He has done for men, is the ground of the prayer; then follows the simple expression of some want of which the heart is conscious — some want which we feel, and yet which seems often to lie too deep for utterance; perhaps it is this very want of the power to tell, or even to know what one is wanting; the result is a petition that God, who desires us to have the good which we cannot grasp, will make His will effectual in spite of our inability, in spite even of our reluctance.

"We are to bring," says the Casuist, "humble and contrite hearts. And, therefore, it must be ascertained what contrition is, and how much of contrition is needful to constitute a true repentance, an acceptable sacrifice." In what delicate scales have men's tears and sorrows been weighed out by divines, to know whether they answered to this standard; how the hearts and consciences of suffering and penitent men have been, not tormented merely — that is nothing — but made utterly insincere and false by their efforts to apply the rules and test their own condition! And vain it is to point out, in mere words, that as long as a man fancies that he has contrition, or any other present, to bring to God, in order to make himself acceptable, so long he is not really humbling himself; he is not confessing that he is a sinner; he is not giving up himself. . . . But God makes this known to a man in *fact;* His discipline brings us to understand it inwardly.

* *

How much has the indifference and listlessness which we witness to do with want of hope! How strenuous, we are sure, some of the laziest people about us might become, if they had but any goal in the distance which might, some day, be reached. If for a moment they do catch sight of such a goal, if they only fancy that they do what a movement there is in the midst of their torpor; how the dry bones shake, are ready almost to come together, to start up, to live! But it seems as if these impulses were to become rarer and rarer. . . . There is a decay

of hope and of all the moral strength which hope
awakens. Men are not content with what they see
about them, far less content with themselves, yet they
do not look for anything higher or better. They do
not think it is worth while to struggle to retain that
which they have, any more than to grasp that which
they have not. . . . There is a sleepy dreary
fatalism into which we are settling down. . . .
We need something more than an earthly or a human
voice to break that slumber, and prevent it from passing into death. I believe that voice is speaking to us.
. . . I need not repeat what I have said to you so
often that *the opening of Heaven* in this book (of
Revelations) and elsewhere in Scripture, does not im-
ply the discovery of a distant or future paradise, but
of the kingdom of God which is in the midst of us;
the divine order which is hidden from the eye, but
apart from which nothing that the eye beholds has any
meaning or substance. What was opened to the Seer
at this time was then, as I believe, the mystery of our
human condition, of the world within us and without
us, of the power which is working for every man and
against every man! . . . of the purpose which
may govern every man's life, of the sure and certain
hope which is set before mankind, a hope of which
every man is an inheritor, if he does not disclaim his
manhood.

**

Let us not be cast down or lose our heart and hope
for anything that we may feel within, any more than
for anything that we may see around us. . . . The
secret of strength, friend and brother, of all moral purpose is to assure thyself that thou art not engaged in
a battle between two portions of thy own nature.   It
is Christ in thee, who is inviting thee, commanding
thee to every brave, and true, and earnest effort.   And
in His commandment is life; what He bids thee to do,
he will enable thee to do. . . . And with moral
purpose will come hope.   When we think of Christ as
a Being at a distance from us — who has merely done
a mighty work; when we eat the bread and drink the
wine in remembrance of an absent Friend, not as
pledges of a near and present one ; the pressure of evil
that crushes down our faith and hope and love seems
to make the past redemption wholly unavailing for our
great necessity.   But *Christ in us*, as St. Paul told the
Colossians, *is the hope of glory*.   What we want is not
that we should attain some separate and selfish bliss,
but that He, who has been striving with us all our lives
through, to deliver us from the separation and selfishness which have been our torment and curse, should finally effect His own purpose . . that we should be His
willing servants; free children of His Father, formed
into one family and body by His blessed Spirit for ever.

**

The Reformers . . . could treat men — not a few here and there with special tastes and tempers of mind — not easy men with plenty of leisure for self-contemplation — but the poorest, no less than the richest, the busiest, no less than the idlest, as spiritual beings, with spiritual necessities, with spiritual appetites, which God's spirit is ever seeking to awaken, and the gratification of which, instead of unfitting them for the common toil of life, is precisely the preparation for it, precisely the means of enabling them to be clear, straightforward, manly; to fulfil their different callings in the belief that each one of them, be it grand or petty, sacred or secular in the vocabulary of men, is a holy calling in the sight of God. But to assert that man is a spiritual being in this sense, you must claim for him a right and power to pray. You must give him a *common prayer* in every sense, of the word, not *special* prayers adapted to special temperaments and moods of character, but human; . . . reaching to the throne of God, meeting the daily lowly duties of man.

The Paternoster is not, as some fancy, the easiest, most natural, of all devout utterances. It may be committed to memory quickly, but it is slowly learnt by heart. Men may repeat it over ten times in an hour, but to use it when it is most needed, to know what it means, to believe it, yea, not to contradict it in the very act of praying it . . . this is hard; this is one of the highest gifts which God can bestow upon us; nor can we look to receive it without others which we may wish for less; sharp suffering, a sense of wanting a home, a despair of ourselves.

*
* *

I think that a priest who . . . invites us to join in a prayer of this kind and then acts as our spokesman and interpreter, bears a better witness for the spiritual condition of man, for his deliverance from the fetters of time and place . . . than that which is borne by those who maintain that worship is only free and comprehensive in woods or upon mountains. Worship there as much as you please; the more, the better. But take care that you do not fly thither to be out of the way of those who live in close alleys, damp cellars, dark garrets. Take care that you are not running from your kind to be easy and comfortable in your own grand thoughts. If you do so, you may worship a spirit of the air, but you will not worship God who is a Spirit. You may exalt yourself, but you will not feel that you are a spirit; for a spirit seeks true fellowship with all other spirits. Churches are not built as signs of exclusion, but of reconciliation.

⁎

At all hazards, in despite of all reasonings, and all authority, cling to the prayer, (*Thy Will be done*). That will never do you harm, or lead you astray. The more we use it, in the faith that the Will we ask should be done is the right, loving and blessed Will, the more we shall know that it is, the more we shall be sure that it must be done. We shall meet every day with a set of new impediments to that conviction; at times it will seem the most monstrous and incredible of all convictions; then when it does, the prayer is specially needed to raise us above the plausible lies of our understandings; to place us in a point of view whence we can see the truth which surmounts them. That point of view is obtained when our state is the lowliest.

⁎

Thought and prayer both come from a hidden source; they go forth to fight with foes and gain victory in the external world; they return to rest in Him who inspired them. Oh! how fresh and original will each of our lives become, what flatness will pass from society, what barrenness from conversation, what excitement and restlessness from our religious acts, when we understand these secrets!—when the morning prayer is really a prayer for grace to One whose service is perfect freedom, in knowledge of whom is eternal life; when at evening we really ask One from whom all

good thoughts and holy desires and just works proceed
for the peace which the world cannot give.

* *

To despair of the present must be bad : to hope for
the future must be good. And this hope our Lord
cherishes and confirms, as much as he disowns that
despair. . . . *"He is not the God of the dead, but
of the living ; for all live unto Him."* What are all
speculations about separate states and intermediate ex-
existences to this celestial sentence ?

* *

Each sorrow is entertained in a different chamber of
imagery ; strikes a different string of the heart. No
wonder, therefore, people ask for special prayers, for
prayers suited to their own cases. Their mistake is
this — they suppose it is possible for them to make, or
for their priests to make, prayers which shall suit their
cases ; and which shall not suit a multitude of cases besides. The individuality is not given by the words
spoken, but by him who speaks them. . . . If they
only touch the specialities of your suffering, they will
not tell what you are suffering ; if they go down far
enough into your experience to be adequate for that
purpose, they will inevitably meet and represent the
thoughts of people whose circumstances, education,
temperament, are altogether unlike yours. The first
simple idea of prayer, which is so apt to be lost in spec-

ulations about its qualities and conditions, that it is a call upon God, who knoweth all things, is the true escape from these and almost all other perplexities.

**
* **

It is an idle fashion of preachers to bid people who have sold themselves to the world, not to love it. They do not love it; their love is all dried up and exhausted. They tell you so. They say, " It is a dreary business altogether; we wish we were fairly out of it; only we do not know what is to come after; that may be worse." Talk not to such men of giving up love. Try whether there is not some object which, even in the midst of their weariness — yes, even because they are so weary,— they may be tempted to embrace. Tell them of a Father's love, which is seeking them out; which has allowed them to wander away from home, and to feel famine and feed upon husks, that they may be driven to seek Him — that so the yoke of the world may be broken from their necks; it never can be broken by exhortations about the vanity of enjoyments which they know much better than the preacher does, to be insipid and insincere. It is the man who is full of the highest, bravest, most godly impulses, who rejoices in the belief that he has a Father in Heaven, and that He is good, and that the world is overflowing with His goodness — it is just he who needs this warning, *" Love not the world"* — needs it, not that the fire in his heart may burn less vehemently; not that he may be chilled with prudential notions; but precisely that the fire may not die out and leave only a few smouldering ashes behind; precisely that he may not sink into a dry, withered, heartless creature, a despiser of all youthful aspirations and hopes.

**

Let us be very careful in understanding the temptation of the age, because it is certainly our own. Let us not think we escape it by doing just the opposite of those who seem to us to have fallen into it; by cultivating all opinions and notions which they reject; by fearing a truth when they speak it. We may find that their practical conclusions meet us at the point which we thought the furthest from them, and that we have turned away from the very principle with which we might have strengthened ourselves, if not have done some good to them. Still less let us refuse to have our own loose and incoherent notions brought to trial, lest in losing them we should lose the eternal truths of God's word. Depend upon it they are in the greatest peril from every insincere habit of mind we tolerate in ourselves; they will come out with a brightness we have never dreamed of when we are made simple and honest. Therefore let us pray this prayer, "*Hallowed be Thy Name*," believing that it has been answered, and being confident that it will be answered.

**
* *

. . . If I have not failed wholly to express the mind of St. John, I have shown you that it is Life we want; that everything is worthless except that. . . . It is the life of a Son, it is filial love, which he de-' sires we should all possess; it is a life which does not exclude one human creature from its blessedness. That we rise into theology when we seek for this life, I have confessed from the first; for theology means the teaching or word concerning God; and St. John's teaching or word concerning God is, that this loving universal life is His; and that He has made us par-takers of it. But if we rise into theology, it is not that we may bring ourselves into a circle of notions, opinions, dogmas; it is that we may escape from them; it is that we may drop the forms and conceits of our mind, as the butterfly drops the chrysalis in which it has been buried.

**
* *

Truth will always seem deeper, broader, higher, the nearer we approach it: the more we converse with the eternal, the less shall we dream of comprehending it. But does not our unrest come from the desire to hold that in the hollow of our hands which holds us; in which we are living? Christ came to deliver us from this unrest. He plunged into the deep waters. They sustained Him: He tells us they will sustain us. The

unfathomable truth of which He bore witness is our
home and dwelling-place. To be in fellowship with
that, is to be perfect, as our Father in heaven is perfect. To be struggling with whatever opposes that, in
ourselves and in our brethren, is to be entering into
Christ's work on earth. This truth . . . is the
same that men in every age have sought and struggled
for. . . . What they wanted, what their inmost
hearts told them must be, was a righteousness and love
without variableness, or the shadow of a turning.
They called it, and call it still, Happiness. What they
want is that which is, beyond all chance or hap, a
Being in whom their being can find its end and aim.
They have climbed up to heaven and gone down to
the deep in search of it. Lo! it is near to them;
their hearts may turn to it and repose in it. They
hoped to find it in some condition of their own minds.
They do find it, when, worn out with their own efforts,
they say, "Thou who art the truth, Thou in whom is
the eternal life, hold us up, for we are Thine."

_

. . . Every gross and cruel superstition has this
origin and definition; it springs from ignorance of the
name of God; it consists in and by that ignorance.
It mixes Him with His creatures; first, with what is
highest in them, next with what is mean, then with
what is basest; finally it identifies Him with the Evil

Spirit. What is darkest and most hateful; what a man flies from most and would desire should not exist; this becomes the object of his worship.

* *
*

During the weeks of Lent, in which we have been hearing of the calamities of other men, or entering into trials of our own, there will have been thoughts put into our minds . . . of some good we might do, some wrong we might redress, some disease that has penetrated into the vitals of our society — the seeds of which we can detect too clearly in ourselves — that we should be assisting to cure. We are too well used, alas! each of us, to see such thoughts in the blossom, and then to see them falling before they ripen further, or nipped by the frost just as they have budded. Experience has made us callous to such sights. But they are unspeakably sad. To help to pave Hell with these half-formed, broken resolutions — should we not strive earnestly that we may not do that?

* *
*

The forty days, which bring the Fasting and Temptation to our mind, are given us especially that we may be taught how to pray this prayer (" *Give us this day our daily bread* "). . . . There are some who know, in their consciences, that they are apt to mock God when they speak these solemn words, apt to take food and every other blessing as if it were their right of which no power in heaven or earth except by sheer injustice can deprive them. Something which shall tell them of dependence, some secret reminiscence, insignificant to others, that all things are not their own; some hint that there are a few million creatures of their flesh and blood who cannot call any of these things their own, is needful for *them.* If it comes in the form of punishment sent specially to themselves, they cannot say it was not wanted; if it is a voice addressed generally to the whole Church, a season returning year by year, they cannot pretend that there are any satisfactory reasons why they should close their ears to it. What they ought to desire is, that they may keep the end in sight; so they will not reckon means, of whatever kind they be, of any value for their own sakes; they will not fancy that to abstain from food is more meritorious in God's sight, than to eat it; if in either case equally, they are desiring to recollect that it is a good which He bestows. Above all, they will feel that, whatever else Lent is, it is certainly a time of confession, and their great hope of being ever able to use this prayer more faithfully must be grounded on an examination of the causes which have made it so unreal in times past.

***

. . . The sublimest teaching may be the most homely . . . the grandest expectations of the future may most cheer us for the toils and sufferings of the present. Our expectations of the future divide us from the present when they are selfish. We are less fit to endure common griefs, to alleviate the griefs of others, when we are desiring blessings which our fellow-men will not share. Nothing can brace us so much to painful effort, to continual patience, as the hope of a revelation of the Universal Deliverer, of an Emancipator of the whole Creation.

* *

Self-willing, self-seeking, self-glorifying, here is the curse: no shackles remain when these are gone; nothing can be wanting when the spirit sees itself, loses itself, in Him who is Light and in whom is no darkness at all. In these words, therefore, (" *Thine is the glory* ") we see the ground and consummation of our prayer; they show how prayer begins and ends in Sacrifice and Adoration. They teach us how prayer, which we might fancy was derived from the wants of an imperfect suffering creature, belongs equally to the redeemed and perfected. In these the craving for independence has ceased; they are content to ask and to receive. But their desire of knowledge and love never ceases.

* *

The Hindoo, in action the idlest, is in imagining, dreaming, combining, the most busy of all human

creatures. . . . Have we not found an assurance
in the mind of these people that all the efforts of
thought in them must originate in a communication
from above, and require fresh communications to meet
them? In the thinking, or reasoning, or religious
faculty, call it what you will, . . . have arisen
desires and longings after converse with the unseen
world, with some living being in the unseen world,
with some one between whom and himself he feels
there is a relation. His religious books echo the cry:
they mutter a half-response to it; but the response is
only the question thrown into a more definite form.
The highest student meditates on the problem, and
repeats his own thoughts; or more probably, what
some ancient person, who meditated and conversed
with the Divinity, said about it. The circle is a very
weary one; if we calmly consider it, and what kind
of comfort those receive who are always revolving in
it, we shall confess that the Hindoo is right in his belief that the wisdom of which he sees the image and
reflection, must speak and declare itself to him; that
he cannot always be left to grope his way amidst
the shadows which it casts in his own mind, or in the
world around him. I ask nothing more than the Hindoo system and the Hindoo life as evidence that there
is that in man which demands a Revelation — that
there is *not* that in him which makes the Revelation.

⁎

— God's will must be the law of the universe. Every creature in the universe must be in a right or wrong position, must be doing his work well, or failing in it, as he yields himself to this will, or as he resists it. And let us not fancy that the early Mahometan was entirely mistaken as to the way in which this will ought to be obeyed. He may not have understood what enemies he had to fight with, what weapons he had to wield, but he did discover that the life of man is to be a continual battle, that we are only men when we are engaged in a battle. He was right that there is something in the world which we are not to tolerate, which we are sent into it to exterminate. First of all, let us seek that we may be freed from it ourselves; but let us be taught by the Mussulman that we shall not compass this end unless we believe, and act upon the belief, that every man and every nation exists for the purpose of chasing falsehood and evil out of God's universe.

⁎

Look at these religions, and you see in them all a witness of unity. Look at them again and you see there is something which divides them from each other. They confess that if men are to unite, it must be in something above themselves; they cannot unite; for **things beneath themselves, the accidents of life, the**

climate, the soil of the lands in which they dwell,
seem to determine what it is that is above them. . .
. This is the report which history gives of these religions, the stamp which they have left of themselves
upon the actual universe. Dare you talk of all this as
merely an illustration of the working of the religious
principle in men? . . . Or can you comfort yourself with saying, " These have all passed away ; the
Persian Ormuzd and Ahriman, — the Egyptian dream
of types in the world which must have some anti-
type,— the Greek question, . . . the Odin warfare
of good and evil spirits ; they have passed away as
visions of the night." Visions they were, but visions
which came to men concerning the dreadful realities of
their own existence. They were visions of the night,
but by them men had to steer their vessels and shape
their course ; without them, all would have been dark.
And we belong to the same race with the men who
had these visions : some nearer to us, some more distant, some . . . almost our kinsmen after the
flesh ; *all* our kinsmen in reality.

We are in a world of action, and energy, and enter-
prise, more unlike that dreaming and speculative world
we have been hearing of than the soil and climate of
England are unlike those of Hindostan. And yet, I
will be bold to say it, the same thoughts which stir the

spirit of the Indian sage and the Indian Sudra, are
working secretly beneath all our bustling life, are af-
fecting the councils of statesmen, are entering into the
meditations of the moralists and metaphysicians who
most despise theology ; in another form are disturbing
the heart of the country peasant, and of the dweller in
St. Giles. They are such questions as these — What
do we worship? A dream or a real Being? One
wholly removed from us, or one related to us? . .
. . What is the evil that I find in myself? Is it myself? . . . What are these desires which I feel in
myself for something unseen, glorious and perfect?
Are they all phantasy or can they be realized? If
they can, by what means? Has He to whom they
point made Himself known to me? How am I connected with Him? Must I utterly renounce all the
things about me that I may be absorbed into Him, or
is there any way in which I can devote them and myself
to Him, and only know Him the better by filling
my place among them? These are the great human
questions: distance in time and space do not affect
them.

* *

It is in prayer you must find the answer (to doubt.)
Yes, in prayer to be able to pray ; in prayer to know
what prayer is. . . . I cannot solve this doubt. I
can but show you how to get it solved. I can but say

the doubt itself may be the greatest blessing you ever
had, may be the greatest striving of God's spirit within
you that you have ever known, may be the means of
making every duty more real to you.

***

This I take to be the first part of the Human or
Universal Worship, — the acknowledgment in whatever
forms of speech, by whatever signs,— the most simple
and universal having most evidence of a divine origin
— of a Will that is absolutely good, of a Will that has
sought and is seeking to make men good. . . .
There is a delight in Truth and Goodness which must
find an expression that is compatible with awe and
reverence ; which, as it shrinks from flattering the
dearest of earthly objects, must be horrified at any
approach to insincerity towards Him from whom their
excellence is derived. To be made true is above all
other things that which you ask of the living and true
Being.

VIII.

FAITH.

THE confidence of a power always at work within us, manifesting itself in our powerlessness, a love filling up our lovelessness, a wisdom surmounting our folly, the knowledge of our own right to glory in this love, power and wisdom, the certainty that we can do all righteous acts by submitting to this Righteous Being, and that we do them best when we walk in a line chosen for us, not of our choosing — this is the strength, surely, and nothing else, which carries us through earth and lifts us into Heaven.

* * *

The Son of God did not *acquire* obedience by taking upon Him our nature. Obedience was His divine nature. He endowed ours with it.

* * *

" *Peace I leave with you* " has always seemed to me nearly the most lovely and blessed sentence in the New Testament. That it should be peace itself — not peace *if our state of mind* is fit to receive it, but the

gift of the state of mind — is very divine. It seems
Christ giving Himself — (indeed, it must be this.)   He
is our Peace.

* *
*

. . . We say to every man, " Believe in the Lord
Jesus Christ, and you shalt be saved." Not believe in
a distant Christ, not believe in a dead Christ ; but believe in the Lord Jesus Christ.   Believe in Him as the
Lord of your own spirit.   Believe that your spirit is as
much His servant as you have believed it the servant
of the flesh.   Believe Him to be mightier than the
world around you, than your own flesh, than the evil
spirit.   Believe and live.

* *
*

Our folly and our misery is, that we do not ask Him
and trust Him to fulfil His promises.   They exceed all
that we can ask or think. . . . In a little time,
when this world and its fashion have passed away from
before our eyes, we shall find that it is so.   We shall
find that we had Him with us all through our pilgrim-
age : that He was every moment speaking to us, and
moving us to do right; every moment warning us of
the wrong.   We shall find that we have erred in hoping
not too much, but far, far too little !   If we had hoped
more, we should have been freer, and purer and more
loving.   We have despaired of God's goodness, therefore it has been far from us.

The Message may come through any man's voice, through the parent, the wife, the child. . . . It may reach us through the letter of a book, or through music, or through a picture. It may be brought to us through the glory of a sunset or the darkness of a night. It may come by fervent expectations or by bitter disappointment, by calm joy, or by intense anguish of body or soul. But the source is ever the same living Word of God.

Very hard indeed it is for a sick person who is tossing on his bed and can find no rest, for a lonely man who has lost himself on the hills at night, to believe that the sun will ever rise. But the sun does rise, and fill the world with his light. So when we feel our own evils, and when we look on all the wrongs and oppressions of the world, we cannot help fancying that the Deliverer is very far away and has forgotten us. But He is not far away; He has not forgotten us. And St. John tells every sufferer, and every man who feels the burden of his sins, how he may find that out. "Abide," he says, "in Christ. . . . Get into the way of asking His help in your troubles: get into the way of asking Him to keep you from doing wrong things and to help you to do what is right."

⁎

When we find out that we have this Friend, this Healer, this Life-giver, so close to us, and that we may turn to Him and confess all that is oppressing us, — all that we are most ashamed of in the past of our lives — when we believe that He is such an one, and that He can understand us, and that He can heal us, then our lives become altogether different. Then we can become simple honest brave men, who do not want to hide anything from our Maker.

⁎

Will anything less than this divine fire, than this Divine Spirit, suffice for our renovation? Will it avail us to talk of the meek and lowly Jesus? Do we not know that we may talk of Him and think ourselves much better for talking of Him, and may boast of our superiority to others who do not know Him, till all meekness and gentleness depart from us?

⁎

. . . I do not think it is right to *expect* trials. When they are to come, God will fit us for them.

⁎

It seems to me that all relations acquire a significance, and become felt as actually living and real, when contemplated in Him, which out of Him, even to the most intensely affectionate, they cannot have. At first each relation seems to be a step in a beautiful

ladder set upon earth and reaching to Him, prefigur-
ing that heavenly relation: and afterwards, if that top
step be apprehended, a descending ladder set in heaven
and reaching to earth.

* *
*

The gift did not depend upon the desciples power of
seeing Him; He had left it with them. . . . It was
a store to which they might have recourse, not in sunny
hours . . . but in times of weariness and desola-
tion. It was a store . . . for their hearts to feed
upon; . . . it was His peace, not theirs.

* *
*

A really right end involves right means. Therefore
our faith must be in a present and living God, not in
any scheme of ours: then He will purge our eyes to
know Him as the God of Truth.

* *
*

It is surely a perilous and almost fatal notion that
Christian men have less to do with the present than
the Jews had, that their minds and their religion are
to be projected into a region after death, because there
only the Divine Presence is dwelling. Is it possible
that this is what the writers of the New Testament
meant when they proclaimed that the Son of God had
taken flesh and become man, and that henceforth the
Lord God would dwell with men and walk with them,
and that they should be His children, and He would

be their Father? Do such words import that the world in which God has placed us has lost some of the sacredness which it had before; . . . that earth and heaven are not as much united as when Jacob was travelling to the land of the people of the east? . . . Surely there must be terrible contradiction in such language, a contradiction which cannot fail to exhibit itself in our practice, to introduce unreality, insincerity, heartlessness into every part of it.

. . . It is easy for any of us to talk about the troubles and sorrows that men pass through in body and mind and spirit. But we shall only sympathize with them, as St. Paul did, when we have his faith and hope.

We know that we will to do right things and, if we only believe that that *will* belongs to Christ, and is that inmost thing that He loves and is fighting for, we shall be able to do what is otherwise impossible.

Oh, if one had to depend upon the state of one's feelings, changes of one's temperament! If God left us to these! But *He is*, and therefore may we trust Him at all times and in all places, and in all moods of mind.

* *

Our eyes are not formed to create light, but to receive it: if they will close themselves to that which is always seeking to open them and illuminate them, *that* is the sentence, — that is the condemnation.

* *

. . . These two thoughts together — the Divine Love perfected and manifested in submission and sacrifice, the human sympathy with all actual sorrows, — seem to me to constitute the mystery of Passion Week.

* *

I am sure that many times I should have sunk utterly under the feeling of utter hopeless vanity of mind, of dreariness in the affections, feebleness in the will, if the words "I believe in the Holy Ghost" had not been given me as an expression of the best thing I could believe in, and that out of which all other belief might come.

* *

It is worse than madness to fall in love with lies; to say they are so pretty that we cannot part with them, to suppose that we have no means of testing the gold and the alloy.

* *

To know God is eternal life; not to know Him is eternal death. That belief, thoroughly and heartily entertained, instead of making us uncharitable, would be the very ground and root of our charity. God is the perfect charity.

* *

"*He who comes that His sheep might have life, and that they might have it more abundantly*," does not teach us to talk of ourselves as His sheep and of other men as having no part in Him. This is the teaching . . . of those who would persuade us that it is a privilege to have a selfish, separate life, — to have selfish, separate rewards. This selfish, separate life is what Christ promises to save us from. The wide, free pastures into which He would lead us are those upon which we can only graze, because we are portions of a flock: the fold into which He would bring us is for those whom He has redeemed from their separate errings and strayings to rest together in Him.

* *

I am sure that, if the Gospel is not regarded as a message to all mankind of the redemption which God has effected in His Son: if the Bible is thought to be speaking only of a world to come, and not of a Kingdom of Righteousness and Peace and Truth with which we may be in conformity or in enmity now: if the Church is not felt to be the hallower of all professions and occupations, the bond of all classes, the instrument of reforming abuses, the admonisher of the rich, the friend of the poor, the asserter of the glory of that humanity which Christ bears, — *we* are to blame, and God will call us to account as unfaithful stewards of His treasures.

***

All false religion proceeds from the notion that man is to make his way up to God by certain acts, or by a certain faith of his, instead of receiving God's witness of Himself, and yielding to His government.

***

The *starting-point* of the Gospel as I read it, is the absolute love of God; the reward of the Gospel is the knowledge of that love.

***

Whitsuntide brings with it such pledges of the continual presence of the Comforter, of a life arising out of death, of fellowship with all in Heaven and all on earth, as must needs make every birthday a beautiful witness and symbol of the new birth of ourselves and of all creation, of the ultimate deliverance of everything that has in it decay or death.

***

I believe . . . that we are really surrounded by all that we have lost. I do not think that we bring them to us by our thoughts and recollections, but that they are present with us, and that we should believe it more if we believed that God was with us.

\   *
                   * *

I suppose we must be trained to understand Christ's doctrine in the same school. Till we have been under His discipline, we shall have the temper of hirelings, counting His work a hardship, expecting to be paid hereafter for consenting to do it. Or else we shall look for instant harvests — for mighty effects to follow at once from the things that we speak — for those fruits which least manifest the calm, patient, loving will of God, and therefore bring no true and inward satisfaction to the spirit of a man. We must learn to see in the seed that same eternal life which is in the perfect flower and fruit — to believe that God will bring the one out of the other: otherwise, we shall have much excitement and much weariness, but no food which can support us, no joy which will connect us with the ages that are past and the ages to come.

                    *
                   * *

The Holy Spirit . . . will not allow us to be satisfied with our advanced knowledge or great discoveries, but will always be showing us things that are *coming:* giving us an apprehension of truths that we have not yet reached. . . . The Spirit leads men away from that incessant poring over the operations, and experiences of their inner life, which is unhealthy and morbid, to dwell upon the events which are continually unfolding themselves in God's world under His providence.

***

That the Kingdom of Heaven is within us, not through some effort of ours to believe in it, but because it has always been — when we knew it and dreamed of it least, — I am more and more convinced. When our Lord said "It is at hand," He surely meant this. He came that He might make us know where it is, and might turn us to it from all the things that have kept us from it, and yet have been illuminated by it.

In one way or another, I fancy, we are all taught, or to be taught, this lesson. Pain, I doubt not . . . is one of the great books out of which it is gathered; but different methods are chosen by the School-Master.

***

"*I saw the Lord also sitting on a throne, and his train filled the temple.*" Some of you may have been watching a near and beautiful landscape in the land of mountains and eternal snows, till you have been exhausted by its very richness, and till the distant hills which bounded it have seemed, you know not why, to limit and contract the view, and then a veil has been withdrawn, and new hills, not looking as if they belonged to this earth, yet giving another character to all that does belong to it, have unfolded themselves before you. This is an imperfect likeness . . . of that revelation which must have been made to the inner eye of the prophet, when he saw another throne than the throne of the house of David, another king than Uzziah or Jotham, another train than that of priests or minstrels in the temple, other winged forms than those golden ones which overshadow the mercy-seat. . . . The kings of the house of David reigned, because that king was reigning, whom God had set upon His holy hill of Zion: because He lived on when they dropped one and another into their graves; because in Him dwelt the light and power by which each might illumine his own darkness, sustain his own weakness. The symbols and services of the temple were not, as priests and people often thought, an earthly machinery for scaling a distant heaven; they were witnesses of a heaven nigh at hand, of a God dwelling in the midst of His people, of His being surrounded by spirits which do His pleasure, hearkening to the voice of His words.

**

. . . It is true of earthly symbols, still more of heavenly visions, that they are meant to carry us out of words and above words; not so that we despise them, or think lightly of them, but that we, seeing the reality of the invisible, may not be greatly disturbed by the processes and conceits of our own minds.

***

If there is a Son of Man, one in whom all human feelings, sympathies, affections, reach their highest point, one from whom they have been derived, . . . then the betrayer of that Son of Man exhibits *the* revolt against these feelings, affections, and sympathies, *the* strife against this love, in which every false friend may read the ground and the possible consummation of his own baseness. . . . Whatever pain and inward anguish any have experienced from the insincerity of those who have eaten their bread and lifted up the heel against them, must have been undergone by Jesus with an intensity proportioned to the intensity of His love. Surely this reflection, if we follow it out, may help us more to such an apprehension of His sufferings, as it is permitted and possible for us to have, than any phrases of pompous rhetoric which put Him at a distance from us, and make us suppose that He did not bear *our* griefs and carry *our* sins.

***

Try to be true thyself; resist the powers which are tempting thee to go through thy acts, common or sacred, as if thou wert a mere machine; hold fast thy faith that God is, and is working when thou seest least of His working, and when the world seems most to be going on without Him; assure thyself that there is an order in the universe when all its movements

seem most disorderly.   So will the things around thee
by degrees acquire a meaning and a purpose.   Those
divine services and sacraments which have partaken
of their insincerity, which have become shadows like
them, will show thee what a truth and substance lies
behind them.

* *

If we are now the sons of God, we may leave Him
to settle what we shall be, in what exercises we shall
be engaged, what special tasks shall be assigned us.
The comfort is to think that He will be the orderer of
us and our ways, and not anyone else; that we may
look forward to do His commandments, hearkening
unto the voice of His words: that it is His will to
break all fetters which hinder us from His free service.

* *

This doctrine of a divine compulsion acting upon
the heart and will of a man, of a wisdom ordaining
every step for him, of a love imposing upon him duties
which of himself he would be least willing to under-
take, bearing him on to sufferings from which he
would most shrink, is the one . . .   which every
minister of Christ and every Christian man must, by
one discipline or another, be taught.

* *

The Old Testament civilization was, I take it,
grounded upon the principle that God has made men

in His image, and that He is not made in theirs: the New Testament civilization upon the ground that the full image of God has been revealed in a Man, and that there is a power going forth to act upon the whole being and nature of men, for the sake of raising them and conforming them to that image.

***

It is true of all symbols that we can know but little of them at first. The experience of life interprets them. And it is the hardest thing of all for us to believe that the Highest must wait upon the lowest; that it is not humility, but pride to refuse the service. Wonderful thought to take in! God must stoop, or man cannot stoop. We must set ourselves up as gods unless we believe that God's glory is shown in doing the lowest offices of a man.

***

I do not think we can exaggerate the blessing that it would be to . . . all of us if we simply accepted the sacrifice of Christ and lived upon it.

***

We say we wish to bring the sinner, weary, heavy-laden and hopeless, to Christ. What can be a more blessed, or more benevolent, or more divine desire? But do we mean that we merely wish to bring the sinner to know what Christ did and spoke, in those thirty-three years between His birth and His resurrection? I fear we shall never understand the infinite significance of those years, or be able to take the Gospel narrative of them simply as they stand, if we have no other thought than this, or if there is no other which we dare proclaim to our fellow-men. Do we not really believe that Christ was, before He took human flesh and dwelt among us? . . . Is this a mere arid dogma . . . which has nothing to do with our inmost convictions, with our very life? How has it become so? Is it not because we do not accept the New Testament explanation of these appearances and manifestations; because we do not believe that Christ is in every man, the source of all light that ever visits him, the root of all the righteous thoughts and acts that he is ever able to conceive or to do?

***

All the Evangelists agree in connecting faith in the subject with most, if not all, these acts of power, (miracles). Now if the miracles were merely, or chiefly, evidences of a divine mission, . . . one would rather have expected that the displays would have been most startling and overwhelming where the unbelief was most obstinate. . . . Whereas, if these signs and powers were but the tokens and manifestations of the presence of One who came to claim the human spirit as His subject, and to raise it out of subjection to other masters, we perceive at once that there is something more regal and more mysterious in an act which calls out the man himself into trust and hope, than in that which merely rectifies the energies of his body or even of his mind. Not only the limb is straightened, not only the issue of blood is staunched, but the person who wields the limb, through whose veins the blood flows, is called into existence and health by the voice of the life-giver.

That righteous King of your heart whom you have felt to be so near you, so one with you, that you could hardly help identifying Him with yourself, even while you confessed that you were so evil, He is the Redeemer as well as the Lord of you and of man. . . . He has taught you that you have been in chains, but that you have been a willing wearer of the chains. To break them, He must set you free. Self is your great prison-house. The strong man, armed, who keeps that prison in safety, must be bound.

. . . We must be content that the knowledge of Him should evolve itself slowly in our minds: we must be thankful if any perplexities and sorrows, from within or from without, prepare us for it. The Name of Him who was born of the Virgin may be familiar to us, it may be surrounded with many beautiful and venerable associations, it may recall moments of youthful tenderness, or remorse, or enthusiasm. And yet it may rather hover about our minds than be rooted in them: we may be trying by acts of memory, or fancy, or strong passionate efforts of what we call faith, to bind it to us more closely. What we want, I think, is to know the barrenness and hollowness of our own selves. If there is not some One beneath ourselves, the ground of all that we desire and believe and are, the spring of our hopes and the consummation of them, the fountain of all love in every creature and the satisfaction of its love, life is a very miserable sleep, full of turbulent, broken dreams.

**

"The *just shall live by his faith.*" There lies the secret of the life of an Israelite; he shall live by his faith. Feeling and knowing himself to be nothing, he is obliged to cast himself wholly upon God. And anything which takes away that self-confidence, and anything which brings forth that faith, is blessed, is divine, let the outward aspects of it be as dark, let the inward anguish which it produces, be as terrible as it may. Here is the solution of the riddles of the universe; here is the key to God's dark and inscrutable ways. Not a solution which we can resort to as if it were a formula of ready application, which may stifle questioning and set our minds at ease. Not a key such as empirics and diviners use, pretending that they know all the wards of every mystery, and can open it at their pleasure, but one to which the humble and meek can always resort when most baffled, when most ignorant.

*

See if the one thought of a living and righteous Being — working amidst the changes of time, working upon human wills for a loving and gracious purpose, working for a purpose which has been realized — does not give you a power of understanding facts which you were content to leave unexplained, does not enable you to bear your ignorance of those which you cannot explain. I do not say that it will be so if you are not convinced that the perfect ideal of Humanity has been brought forth; that a Man, who perfectly submitted that the clay which He bore should be moulded according to the will of an Almighty Father, is the centre of Human Life, Society, History. But I am sure, if that faith is fully received into your hearts that the weary maze will become a blessed order, and that you will think of the condition of your race and of its members with a sympathy and a hope which . . . only the God of Sympathy and Hope and Consolation can bestow.

*

When I began in earnest to seek God for myself, the feeling that I needed a deliverer from an over-

whelming weight of selfishness was the predominant
one in my mind. . . . I thought He was just that
Being who was exhibited in the cross of Jesus Christ.
If I might believe His words, " *He that hath seen me
hath seen the Father;* " if, in His death, the whole
wisdom and power of God did shine forth, there was
one to whom I might fly from the demon of Self,
there was one who could break his bonds asunder.
That was and is the ground of my Faith.

✲✲

In the sad hours of your life, the recollection of that
Man you read of in your childhood, the Man of Sorrows, the great sympathizer with human woes and
sufferings, rises up before you: it has a reality for you
then: you feel it to be not only beautiful, but true.
In such moments, does it seem to you that Christ was
merely a person who, eighteen hundred years ago,
made certain journeyings between Judea and Galilee?
Can such a recollection fill up the blank which some
present grief, the loss of some actual friend, has made
in your hearts? It does not, it never did this for any
one! Yet I do not doubt for a single instant, that a
comfort has come to you from that contemplation. So
far from denying your right to it, I would wish you
and all earnestly to believe how strong and assured
our right to it is. In Him, and for Him, we were created; this is our doctrine, or rather the doctrine of

St. Paul. . . . If so, is it wonderful that He should speak to you, and tell you of Himself? And oh! if that voice says, "You may trust me, you may lean upon me, for I know all things in heaven and earth — *I and my Father are one,*" is the whisper too good to be true, too much in accordance with the timid antici- pations and longings of our spirits *not* to be rejected?

*_**

When we are ashamed of our strifes, of our indif- ference, of our vainglory, of our money-worship, when we have asked God to put these away from us, to give us true hearts, and to write His name and the name of the Holy City upon us; we shall understand how our fathers saw some letters of that name in every part of the universe. . . . But we shall believe, not be- cause of their word, but because we have seen for our- selves; because we have the Kingdom of God within us: because we have Christ Himself to interpret the parables of it.

*_**

No one, I believe, has ever doubted that the old garment and the old bottles referred to the institutions of the ancient economy; the new garment and the new bottles, to those which Christ would establish. Every one has seen that, in some way or other, our Lord meant to say, that it would be mischievous merely to re-enact the forms and customs which had

belonged to the past, until the substance and the life,
of which customs and forms are the outside, had been
brought out and revealed. But surely, if His Kingdom
were not the everlasting Kingdom which all Jewish institutions had been imperfectly exhibiting, these comparisons and the argument which is founded upon
them would not hold good. He would be substituting
new bottles for the old, not expressing the wine which
was to fill the bottles. No more beautiful illustration
could be conceived of the assertion that the Kingdom
of God, when it had once unfolded itself, would work
out a drapery fitted for itself, and that it would not
merely make use of that drapery which belonged to it
when it was yet undeveloped.

*
* *

Every variation in the story of the Agony is de-
serving of the most careful observation and reflection.
. . . I have nothing to add to what thousands have
said of it; and it is after all what has not been said of
it, the unuttered, unutterable experience of human beings in all kinds and states of suffering for eighteen
hundred years, which has brought out its meaning. I
think I might safely leave it to that experience to declare whether the word "Father" has not been felt to
contain the very essence of the sorrow and the consolation. . . . The intensity of the sorrow is surely
in this, that it is filial sorrow, the distinct will of the

Son coming forth as if it were something separate and alone, yet striving in the agony of prayer to submit itself — to claim its perfect essential unity with the Father's will. . . . Who does not feel that the very secret of the power and life of the Gospel is lying there?

**
**

I find some spirits in different places of this earth very miserable, and others in a certain degree of blessedness. I do not find that the place in which they are makes the difference. . . . I should conclude from these observations, if I had nothing else to guide me, that the moral and spiritual condition of the inhabitants is the means of making a heaven or a hell of this earth. Scripture sustains this conclusion. All it tells me of the Kingdom of Heaven shows me that man must anywhere be blessed, if he has the knowledge of God and is living as His willing subject: everywhere accursed, if he is ignorant of God and at war with Him.

**
**

(The Apostles') prayer for an increase of Faith, plausible as it sounded, Our Lord seems to tell us was itself mixed with covetous desires, which are the great antagonists of faith ; they wanted to have a great amount of faith, not that they might serve God with it, but themselves. They wanted faith as a something upon which they could plume themselves, and which would set them above others: they must learn that God gives men faith that they may do His work, not that they may have a feast of their own.

*

Evil must be denounced at all hazards, and that which is wrong in the tendencies of a time can only be effectually resisted by the assertion of the right which is most akin to it. This is faith and (those who hold it) are in the true sense "just by faith." Their outward acts proceed from a principle; that principle is Trust in an unseen Person.

*

Each of us is disposed to fix upon some one of our Lord's statements, as that to which he shall refer all the rest. If we desire to have our thoughts orderly, not loose and incoherent, . . . there must be a centre round which they revolve. But it is unspeakably important that we should not choose this centre and so create a system for ourselves; but that we should find it. . . . Will anyone say that I am wrong if I affirm that God himself is the centre here, that the Love with which He loved the world is that to which our Lord is leading us, that if we learn from Him what that love is . . . we shall be in a better condition to apprehend all that He is teaching us respecting the birth from above?

***

I plead for the Love of God, which resists sin and triumphs over it, not for a mercy which relaxes the penalties of it. With continual effort, only by the help of that revelation of God which is made in the Gospel of Christ, I am able to believe that there is a might of Good which has overcome Evil. . . . To maintain this conviction, to believe in the Love of God, in spite of the appearances which the world presents and the reluctance of my own nature, I find to be the great fight of life. . . . I admire unspeakably those who can believe in the Love of God and can love their brethren in spite of the opinion which they seem to cherish, that He has doomed them to destruction. I am sure that their faith is as much purer and stronger than mine, as it is than their own system. . . . I do not call upon them to deny anything they have been wont to hold; but I call upon them to join us in acknowledging God's Love and His redemption first of all, and then to consider earnestly what is or is not compatible with that acknowledgment.

***

If we believed that there had been a Spirit of Truth, not acting upon the surface of men's minds, but carrying on a controversy with them in their inmost being, encountering all the rebellions of the cowardly, reluctant Will, all its desire to become a mere Self-will,

bringing out its darkness, as light always must, into
fuller and stronger relief ; . . . if we could believe
that this was a Comforter, a Divine Person, stronger
than His enemies, able to strengthen man to all fixed
resolutions and noble purposes; . . . able to in-
spire longings and hopes when the spirit of man is most
bent and cowed; able to point him upward to a
Father in Heaven when he is most ready to call himself only a son of earth ; able at the same time to make
him understand his work on earth, and to endow him
with powers for performing it ; able to support him in
suffering ; to give him glimpses of the substantial glory
into which Christ has entered through suffering; able
to make him perceive that everything which is merely
his own is perishable, that what is most divine is common to him with his fellows ; — then I think we need
not choose the bright spots of modern history and conceal its horrors ; the more courageously we face the one,
the more hope will come to us from the contemplation
of the other.

* *

. . . Why have the sects . . . become so
· partial, so hard, so cruel? Is it because their forefathers were wrong in telling them that the Spirit was
seeking to bind them in one, and that no mere external bond could bind them ? Surely not ; this lesson,
taken home to the heart, makes men first true, in due

time Catholic, leading them to cling mightily to the
special conviction God has wrought in them, afterwards enabling them to feel the necessity of other convictions to sustain that. It is the *loss* of this faith, it
is the substitution of some petty external badge and
symbol of theirs, for the belief and confession of a
Divine Spirit, which is making them impatient of
dogmas, yet fiercely dogmatic; eager to rob other men
of their treasures; feeble in their hold upon their own.

**

The Church does not maintain in one prayer, but in
all its prayers, that the love of God is the only root and
ground of Christ's Atonement and that the perfect
submission of the Son to the will of the Father consti-
tutes the deepest meaning of the Sacrifice. These
principles belong to the essence of our faith.

**

You cannot trust God too much. You cannot be
too confident that He is guiding you, and that every
embarrassment in your thoughts, every complication in
your circumstances, is known by Him, is intended by
Him as a means to enable you to understand wisdom
secretly, that you may show forth the fruits of it
openly. . . . Faith in the righteousness of God
gives you that prudence or providence which will
make you wary of your footsteps, suspicious of yourselves. Faith in the righteousness of God gives you

that courage which will enable you to move on steadily, calmly, resolutely, certain that you will have light
to see what you ought to do, and that, in doing it,
you will know more of the just and gracious mind of
God towards all men as well as towards yourselves.

**

. . . Seeing what appear to us the most irregular
currents obey a fixed and eternal law, we may be sure
that that Spirit of Truth will work as He has always
worked; that He will change nothing and yet will make
all things new. That mighty wonder which we behold
every year when the self-same roots and stems, which
were the symbols of all that is hard and dry and separate become clothed with verdure, full of life and joy
and music, will be exhibited in the moral world. No
form will be cast away, no ordinance will be treated as
worthless, nothing which has expressed the thought or
belief of any man will be found unmeaning, because the
Spirit of the living God will call forth every sleeping
and latent power into activity, everything that has
been dead into life ; all that has been divided into harmony. Only the miserable counterfeits will pass away.
Whatever has been true, if it has been ever so weak
and broken, will find its place.

**

Everyone must, I think, at some moment of his life,
have been startled by the wonderful force of the words

in Scripture with which he has been most familiar and
which had seemed to him most commonplace. For
instance the word "*trust*" which meets us at every
turn in the Book of Psalms. In overwhelming troubles, in a time of utter weariness, when every calculation has been disappointed, when there seems no fair
ground for expecting help from any quarter, when all
is dark within and without, how has this little word
dawned upon a man, what a witness it has seemed to
give of a world of light somewhere, perhaps not far off!
. . . To fear God he knew was right, whether he
did it, or no; to love God he had always held to be
right, if it were possible. But to trust in God, without being certain that he does either fear or love; to
trust because all is in God which he has not and feels
he has not, in himself, this is precisely what he needs,
and precisely to this the book . . . is inviting
him.

⁂

The expression . . . that the Son of God reconciled the Father to us, has pained many who have seen
the unmeasurable importance of recognizing all love as
proceeding from the Father, and having its root in
Him. . . . If the idea of satisfaction as the fruit
of Love, as the image of Love in the Son, answering
to the archetype of it in the Father, were filling our
minds, there would be no difficulty in admitting the

assertion that the Son reconciled the Father to us.
He presented that perfect reflex of His own character to
the Father, with which He alone could be satisfied. In
Him only could He see Humanity as He had formed it,
with all its powers in full exercise, free and glorious, —
free and glorious because entirely submissive to love.
. . . Christ alone offered himself a complete sacrifice, not to necessity, not to the tyranny of Death, but to
Love. He had power to lay down His life. He gave
it up. Wherein had all creatures failed? Simply in
this: they had not trusted God. They had not yielded
themselves to Him, relying upon His love, casting
themselves unreservedly upon it. . . . Self divided
their hearts with love, sometimes wholly vanquished it.
. . . None ever showed forth His whole character;
none ever sympathized with the whole human kind,
and with each member of it; none ever felt towards
their brethren as the Father of all felt to them.
Therefore none of them could destroy the separation
between God and His creation. . . . Only the Son
could reconcile the Father to men; could make humanity wholly acceptable to a wholly loving Being. But
was this reconciliation a change of His mind? Did it
make His character other than it was before, or His
feelings towards our race more gracious? No; for the
very complacency of God was for this, that His character could now first be seen in One who bore our nature;

that His purposes of grace to us could now first be accomplished in One who called us brethren.

**

There is an abstract way of thinking about the Son of God, which is hurrying some of us into Pantheism. . . . There is a popular way of thinking about the Son of God, which is hurrying us into idolatry. . . . Nor do I see how either evil can be averted if we do not more earnestly consider what is involved in the faith of little children. . . . If we were forced to form conceptions about a Son of God, or Son of Man, there would be a perpetual strife of intellects; there could be no consent; each man must think differently from his neighbor, must try to establish his own thought against his neighbor's. If He is revealed to us as the ground of our intellects, — the creative Word of God from whom they derive their light; as the centre of our fellowship, the only-begotten Son of God, in whom we are made sons of God, the weary effort is over: our thoughts may travel to the ends of the earth, but here is their home; apart from Him men have infinite disagreements; in Him they have peace.

**

Instead of picturing to ourselves some future bliss, calling that Eternal Life, and determining the worth of it by a number of years, or centuries, or milleniums, we are bound to say once for all: "This is the eternal life, that which Christ has brought with Him, that which we have in Him, the knowledge of God; the entering into His mind and character, the knowing Him as we only can know any person, by sympathy, fellowship, love."

***

Sacrifice is the common root and uniting bond and reasonable explanation of all those acts which seem in the eyes of men, often in the eyes of those who perform them, most hostile to each other, but which God sees to be essentially alike. . . . But Sacrifice cannot have this ennobling and mysterious power — it will be turned into self-glory and lose its own nature, . . . if it is not contemplated as all flowing from the nature of God; if it is not referred to Him as its author as well as its end.

***

We often make a great and painful effort to realize, as we call it, our Lord's sufferings, to think how transcendently great they must have been, hoping in that way to kindle our sorrow and devotion. The result, I think, is generally disappointment. We rarely work ourselves up to the point we wish; if we do, there comes a strong reaction afterwards. The Church teaches us to avoid such carnal struggles. It is humility we want, not exaltation. It is in submission to

love, not in striving to understand it, and to measure
its workings, that we enter into our Lord's mind, and
follow His example. The person who most simply
confesses his own want of charity, and desires to rest
himself and all upon the infinite Charity of God . . .
will see most into the divine meaning of the Passion.

The curse which the Law pronounced upon men
was death, death in its most odious, most criminal
shape; and He underwent it, an actual, not a fantastic
crucifixion, — the sentence of the rebel and the slave.
Do you ask how this act effected the purpose of re-
deeming any, or how many were included in the
benefits of it? The question is, indeed, most difficult,
if by redemption you understand *in any sense* the deliverance of man out of the hand of God, the pro-
curing a change in His purpose or will; then there is
need of every kind of subtle explanation to show how
the means correspond to the end. But if you suppose
that it is the spirit of a man which needs to be emancipated, a spirit fast bound with the chains of its own
sins and fears, then I do not see what proof, save one,
can be of any avail, that a certain scheme of redemption is effectual. . . . If the spiritual bondage is
not real, of course the spiritual redemption is not real.
But the whole history of the world, of every portion
of the world, for six thousand years, proclaims that it

is real. . . . If the way of deliverance from it has
been found out in some corner of the world, civilized
or uncivilized . . . then let us know the way, let
us try it. But the sacrifices that ascend from ten
thousand altars to powers of sky and earth and air,
. . . declare: "We have not found it; we never
shall till you can tell us of some sacrifice which shall
be of God; one which proceeds from His will and not
ours; one which fulfils His will and not ours." It is
such an one of which St. Paul speaks when he declares that " *Christ has redeemed us from the curse of
the Law, having become a curse for us.*"

**

Is it nothing to think, that every true and faithful
man who has ever wrestled with his own evil, and with
the evil of his brethren . . . has been Christ's
soldier, cheered by His voice; inspired by His spirit?
Is it nothing to think that you have seen but the beginning of their warfare, — when they were just learning the use of their arms and wielding them very
awkwardly; but that now they have entered upon a
new stage of their service, and have profited by their
sorrowful experience and many failures, and rule the
things to which they often yielded subjection, and
confess and obey the Leader, from whose yoke they
so often broke loose? Is it nothing to believe that
now they appreciate each other better, and are not mis-

led by appearances, and are not separated by hard thoughts, but feel that a common bond unites them, that the same banner is over them, and that they have been purified by the same blood from the vain wishes and petty vanities which kept them asunder? Is it nothing to think that now they understand us and sympathize with us as they could not do before; because, if they are more awake to our evils, they are more earnest to deliver us from them; and because they see us no longer as separate from Him who has loved them and us and given Himself for us? . . . Do not conceive of them as dwelling in some distant, unknown region, where they possess some felicity from which you are excluded. Think of them as still caring for the earth, and for the country, and village, and homestead in which they learnt their lessons of humility and trust; think of them as struggling that these may become fit habitations for Righteousness and Peace to dwell in.

* *

We speak scornfully and disparagingly of this earth as if it were a fit place for poor fallen wicked creatures to inhabit; but as if those whom the Spirit makes meet for the Kingdom of Heaven were to look down upon it; at best to regard it only as a place in which they are compelled for threescore years and ten to dwell. These words stand out often in the strong-

est contrast to the acts of those who use them . . .
especially their devotion to the earth's money, the love
of which is said to be the root of all evil. And so I
believe it must be, more and more, if we are not taught
reverence for the earth as an article of faith ; if it is
not declared to us more and more, that the Bible commands this reverence, gives us the strongest and most
sacred reasons for it. . . . The earth, so the old
Hebrews believed, is a grand and awful place, which
God has created and cared for and pronounced very
good. . . . St. Peter believed that the earth had
been made evil by those who inhabited it, just because
they did not recognize its relation to, and dependence
upon, the Kingdom of Heaven.

***

. . . Mahometanism can only thrive while it is
aiming at conquest. Why? Because it is the proclamation of a mere Sovereign, who employs 'men to
declare the fact that he is a Sovereign, and to enforce
it upon the world. It is not the proclamation of a
great moral Being who designs to raise his creatures
out of their sensual and natural degradation ; who reveals to them not merely that He is, but *what* He is —
why He has created them — what they have to do
with Him. Unless this mighty chasm in the Mahometan doctrine can be filled up, it must wither day by
day — wither for all purposes of utility to mankind.

*
* *

You have found a set of men brought up in circumstances altogether different from yours, holding
your faith in abhorrence, who say in language the
most solemn and decisive, " Whatever else we part
with, this is needful to us and to all human beings —
the belief that God *is* — the recognition of Him as a
living personal Being." . . . Be sure that here is
something which the heart and reason within you have
need of — which they must grasp. Be quite sure that,
if you give them in place of it any fine notions or
theories; if you feed them with phrases about the
beautiful or the godlike when they want the source
of beauty, the living God; if you entertain them with
any images or symbols of art or nature when they
want that which is symbolized, if you talk about physical laws when they want the lawgiver, . . . you
are cheating yourselves — cheating mankind.

*
* *

If we use all arguments of fear, all arts of rhetoric,
to convince beggars or princes that they ought to take
care of their souls, a few may be startled out of a sleep
to which they will return again. But the more part
will feel that you are setting them upon a task which
they cannot perform; . . . that you are bidding
them forget the real earth for the sake of a heaven
which they can only dream of. But if, throwing aside

these metaphysics about the soul, we will recur to the
old and simple scriptural phraseology — the phraseology of the hearth and the home — if we will bear
witness to men of a Father who has sent the elder
Brother of the household to bring them into it, to restore them to the place of sons and daughters, to endow them with the highest rights of children — if we
will condescend to this venerable mode of speech, —
we shall find, I believe, that it is not obsolete,   .   .   .
but that it has a power which time and place have
not affected, that it can bring forth as clear a response
from the peasant and mechanic of the nineteenth century, as from the peasant and mechanic of the first.
The strength is in the tidings themselves, not in the
person who delivers them.

* ***

The kingdom of light is mightier than the kingdom
of darkness. This was the substance of the Persian
faith, to the revival of which, in all its strength and
simplicity, all that was vigorous in the Persian character and government seems to have been owing.
There was the greatest difference between it and
the Hindoo — precisely this difference. The Hindoo
thought of light and darkness as the opposition between cultivation and ignorance — between the Brahmin and the Sudra; the Persian looked upon them as
expressions for right and wrong. Far less refined and

intellectual than the Indian, far less capable of mere speculation, he had a sense of practical, moral distinctions to which the other was almost a stranger. . .

. Hence a difference in their scheme of life.

***

Whatever is false is feeble and the cause of feebleness; whatever is truth must come forth and vindicate its might before the Universe. We need that conviction if we would understand the past; we need it for the work of every day; we shall hold it more firmly when we look back upon our present existence from that which is to come.

GENERAL INDEX.

SUBJECTS.

A

B

C

H

O

P

S

NEW PUBLICATIONS.

CHIPS FROM THE WHITE HOUSE.—12 mo. 486 pp. $1.50
What the press says of it:

In this handsome volume of five hundred pages have been
brought together some of the most important utterances of
our twenty presidents, carefully selected from speeches and
addresses, public documents and private correspondence,
and touching upon a large variety of subjects.— *Golden*
Rule, Boston.

Most of the extracts are dated and accompanied by brief
explanations of the circumstances under which they were
written, and the volume, therefore, if judiciously read, will
give a clearer idea of the character of the men than can be
gathered elsewhere by reading a small library through.—
New York Graphic.

The selections are made with judgment and taste, and
represent not only the political status of the distinguished
writers, but also their social and domestic characteristics.
The book is interesting in itself, and specially valuable as
a convenient book of reference for students of American
history. Its mechanical presentation is all that can be
asked.— *Providence Journal.*

Each chapter is prefaced by a brief synoposis of the life
and services of its subject, and most of the extracts are dated,
with brief explanations of the circumstances under which
they were written. The work, in fact, is a handbook. It
is convenient for reference of American history. It is
printed in clear, large type, is tastefully and strongly bound,
and is supplemented by a very full index.— *Woman's Jour-*
nal, Boston.

The book is thoroughly good ; none better could be
placed in the hands of young persons. By the light of
these they can see the reflection of the character of the
grand men who have been called to rule over the Nation
during its existence. No other nation ever had such a
succsssion of rulers, where so few have proved failures.—
Inter Ocean. Chicago.

NEW PUBLICATIONS.

THE YOUNG FOLKS' BIBLE HISTORY. By Charlotte M. Yonge. Boston: D. Lothrop & Co. Price $1.50. The present volume is not only important in itself, but it is an additional proof of the wonderful versatility of the author. The same hand that so successfully set before young readers the stories of the growth and development of the different countries of Europe, here puts the grand old Bible story into a form which the youngest readers can easily comprehend. The language is simple and the facts are told in modern style; one great stumbling-block to the understanding being thus removed. Beginning with the account of the creation, succeeding chapters carry along the Scriptural record to the time of the prophets, and from their day down to the appearance of the Saviour upon the earth. The life and teachings of Jesus are especially dwelt upon. The volume is profusely illustrated with drawings by English artists. We cannot too cordially commend the plan of this work, nor the excellent manner in which it is carried out. It will be found not only valuable for home teaching, but for use in the infant classes of Sunday-schools.

The New York *Tribune* in a notice of Amanda B. Harris's "How We Went Birds'-nesting" says: "It is written with charming simplicity of style, and its ornithology is taken directly from nature and not from books. There is something of the spirit of adventure in the book, and as the youthful reader of dime novels is filled with a desire to go out West and hunt Indians, so the boys and girls who read this little volume will be prompted to visit the haunts of the birds and will have their powers of observation directed and sharpened."

THE OLD OAKEN BUCKET. By Samuel Woodworth. Quarto Holiday edition. Boston: D. Lothrop & Co. Price $1.50. Of all the illustrated quarto presentation books yet issued, this is by all odds the most artistic and tasteful. The art of the designer, engraver and printer has in turn been exhausted to bring it as near perfection as possible. The drawings are from the skilful pencil of Miss Humphrey, and represent her best work. The engraving is by W. N. Closson, whose reputation in that line is equal to that of any other man in the country, and the printing is from new type on heavy paper with broad margins and gilt edges. In general style and binding the volume is uniform with *The Ninety and Nine, Drifting*, etc.

THE STORY OF FOUR ACORNS. By Alice B. Engle. Ill. Boston: D. Lothrop & Co. Price $1.00. Children who like fairy stories will find in this handsome volume a fountain of delight. The author possesses rare talent for interesting the young, and has here turned it to the best advantage. She has furnished a fascinating story, and has ingeniously woven into it bits of poetry and song from famous authors which will find easy entrance into the mind and create an appetite for more. The illustrations are among Miss Lathbury's best, and do their part toward making the volume attractive.

A capital idea is represented in the new book, *Historic Pictures*, suggested by the success of last season's volume, *Write Your Own Stories*. It consists of a collection of pictures illustrating places and events of historic interest, thirty in number, with three blank pages after each picture, which are to be utilized by the boys and girls in writing an account of the incidents which have made the various places famous. The publishers offer a series of cash prizes for competitors, the lists to remain open until July 1, 1882. The one who sends the best series of stories or historical descriptions of the pictures, will receive $25.00 ; the author of the second best, $15.00, and the third in point of excellence, $10.00.

THE TEMPTER BEHIND. By the Author of " Israel Mort,
Overman." Boston: D. Lothrop & Co. Price $1.25. Most
readers of fiction will remember " Israel Mort, Overman," a
book which created several years ago a profound sensation
both in this country and in England. It was a work of intense strength and showed such promise on the part of the
anonymous author that a succeeding work from the same
hand has ever since been anxiously looked for, in the belief
that, should it be written, it would make a yet more decided
impression. "The Tempter Behind," now just brought out
in this country, shows that the estimate of the public as to
the ability of the author was not too high. It is in every
way a higher and stronger work, and one that cannot but
have a marked effect wherever it is read. It is not merely an
intensely interesting story; something more earnest than
the mere excitement of incident underlies the book. It is
the record of the struggles of a young and ambitious student
against the demon of drink. He is an orphan — the ward of
a rich uncle who proposes to settle his entire property upon
him in case he conforms to his wishes. It is the desire of
the uncle that he shall become a clergyman, a profession for
which the young man has a strong and natural preference.
Unknown to his uncle, he has formed the habit of social
drinking at college from which he cannot extricate himself.
The terrible thirst for intoxicants paralyses his will, and
renders him a slave to the cup. Every effort he makes is
unsuccessful. He loses rank at college, and is afterward
dismissed from his post as private secretary to an official of
the government, on account of the neglect of his studies and
duties, but without exposure. His uncle knows his failures,
but not their cause, and demands that he either enter the
ministerial profession for which he has prepared himself, or
leave the shelter of his roof. The young man, who has too
much principle to assume a position which he fears he may
disgrace, does not confide in his uncle, and secretly departs
from the house, leaving behind him a letter of farewell, determined to make one more trial by himself, and among
strangers, to break the chains which bind him so closely.
The story of his experiences, trials and temptations are viv-
idly and almost painfully told, with their results. The book

NEW PUBLICATIONS.

THE ONLY WAY OUT. By Mrs. Jennie Fowler Willing. Illustrated. Boston: D. Lothrop & Co. Price $1.50. The rather enigmatical title of the handsome volume before us is fully explained in the closing chapter of the story. The author endeavors to show that there is but one sure way out of the darkness into which we are plunged by earthly crosses and trials, and that is an earnest faith in and reliance upon Christ. The lesson sought to be conveyed is mainly through the experience of Joseph Graydon, a bright generous-hearted young merchant, who is cursed with an appetite for liquor so strong that when temptation comes he has no power to resist it. Pledges, promises and resolutions made in his sober moments avail nothing when attacked by the terrible desire for drink. In all his struggles with the habit which is steadily working his ruin, he seeks no help outside of himself, depending only upon his own strength of will to overcome the tempter. He falls at last, a victim to his weakness and blindness in refusing to look for aid whence all aid comes. Says one of the characters in commenting upon his fate — "They may talk as they will, it takes a solid basis of rocky conviction to hold one to this work of mastering the evil that is rampant in the world. You may pile up figures and facts, pathos and argument, but unless God touches the conscience you can't depend upon a man for a steady pull through the breakers. All real reformatory power is vested in the Lord Jesus Christ."

SO AS BY FIRE. By Margaret Sidney. Ill. Boston: D. Lothrop & Co. Price $1.25. Anything from the author of "Five Little Peppers" will be read with eagerness and with the certainty beforehand that it will be well worth reading. *So as by Fire* is a story full of earnest purpose. The lesson it teaches is that it is only through great sorrow and tribulation that some souls are purified; that the trials and vexations and disappointments of this world, if rightly accepted and turned to use, make clean the heart "as by fire." To impress this fact strongly upon the mind of the reader is the constant aim of the author. It is not a child's book, although some of the more entertaining characters in its pages are children. Its purpose is to strengthen those who are bowed down by trouble, and to inspire them with faith in the final reward of constant well doing.

NEW PUBLICATIONS.

ROUND THE WORLD LETTERS. By Lucy S. Bainbridge. Boston: D. Lothrop & Co. Price $1.50. A bright, fresh book of travel, written in a gossipy, unconventional style, and brimful of interest from cover to cover. The author is the wife of a well-known Baptist clergyman of Providence, R. I., W. F. Bainbridge, a lady of culture and observation, and possessed of a fund of humor which gives an agreeable flavor to her book. Mr. and Mrs. Bainbridge left Providence on the first day of January, 1879, for San Francisco, reaching that city in time to study its lions and take the steamer *Tokio* for Japan February 18. At Yokohama they spent two weeks, and at Tokio three, and then set out upon a journey to the interior, visiting a number of the lesser towns and cities. From Japan they sailed for Shanghai, which city they reached two days before the arrival of Gen. Grant. Mrs. Bainbridge gives a very spicy account of the reception of the General and the doings during his stay. The stay in China is even longer than that in Japan. From Hong Kong they sail for Singapore, a journey of fifteen hundred miles, make a tour through southern India, visiting Calcutta, Benares, Lucknow, Delhi and Cawnpore. After India comes Egypt and the pyramids, then the Holy Land ; then Cyprus, Rhodes, Smyrna and Greece; then Venice, Bavaria, Switzerland, France, England and home. It will be seen that the book covers untrodden ground for the most part, and where it does fall into the beaten track the treatment is so original as to make it as interesting as if the same things had never been described before. We commend the volume to readers as a model of what a story of travel should be.

HOME AND SCHOOL SONGS. By Louis C. Elson. Quarto, illustrated, cloth, $1.00. Boston : D. Lothrop & Co. In this volume of songs, the composer has endeavored to give a series of bright and singable melodies for children, which shall be absolutely free from the trashiness which has characterized much of this school of work. The songs have been written with a view to make them quite within the register of all young voices. The subjects are all well-adapted to their purpose, many of them admitting of action, and are suited to the family circle as well as for public schools. Both words and music are the work of Mr. Elson, whose previous efforts in various musical fields are widely known.

NEW PUBLICATIONS.

A BOOK OF GOLDEN DEEDS, OF ALL TIMES AND LANDS. Gathered and narrated by Charlotte M. Yonge. Illustrated. Boston: D. Lothrop & Co. Price $1.25. The rapidly increasing popularity of this little volume, and the steady demand for it have induced the Messrs. Lothrop to bring out a new edition in handsome form and yet at a price which brings it within the reach of every reader. Excellent as are all Miss Yonge's books, there is not one which appeals so strongly to young readers as this collection of stories and traditions, gathered from many sources, and presented for the purpose of inculcating a love for what is noble and true in the minds of the young. The author's intention has been to make it a treasury, where may be found minuter particulars than are given in abridged histories, of the soul-stirring deeds that lend life and glory to the record of events, in the trust that example may inspire the spirit of heroism and self-devotion, and give proof that the highest object of action is not to win promotion, wealth or success, but simple duty, mercy and loving-kindness. Miss Yonge has chosen from history some of the most remarkable instances of moral and physical bravery, and has clothed them in language befitting her theme. Many of them are familiar, but we have never before seen them rendered in so charming a form, or in a manner where the true motive of action was so plainly and effectually brought out. The volume is printed in clear type, on good paper, and is attractively bound.

FIVE LITTLE PEPPERS; and How They Grew. By Margaret Sidney. Thirty-six illustrations by Jessie Curtis. Boston: D. Lothrop & Co. Price $1.50. Of all the new juveniles in this season's list there is not one which will be read with more delight by the little ones than this jolly story. It is a genuine child's book, written by one who understands and sympathizes with children. The incidents are just such as might have happened, and pathos and humor are skilfully mingled in their telling. The illustrations are charming, and worthy the reputation of the artist.

"PANSY" BOOKS.

Probably no living author has exerted an influence upon the American people at large, at all comparable with Pansy's. Thousands upon thousands of families read her books every week, and the effect in the direction of right feeling, right thinking, and right living is incalculable.

Each volume 12mo. Cloth. Price, $1.50.

FOUR GIRLS AT CHAUTAUQUA. MODERN PROPHETS.
CHAUTAUQUA GIRLS AT HOME. ECHOING AND RE-ECHOING.
RUTH ERSKINE'S CROSSES. THOSE BOYS.
ESTER RIED. THE RANDOLPHS.
JULIA RIED. TIP LEWIS.
KING'S DAUGHTER. SIDNEY MARTIN'S CHRISTMAS.
WISE AND OTHERWISE. DIVERS WOMEN.
ESTER RIED "YET SPEAKING." A NEW GRAFT.
LINKS IN REBECCA'S LIFE. THE POCKET MEASURE.
FROM DIFFERENT STAND- MRS. SOLOMON SMITH.
THREE PEOPLE. [POINTS. THE HALL IN THE GROVE.
HOUSEHOLD PUZZLES. MAN OF THE HOUSE.
AN ENDLESS CHAIN.

Each volume 12mo. Cloth. Price, $1.25.

CUNNING WORKMEN. MISS PRISCILLA HUNTER and
GRANDPA'S DARLING. MY DAUGHTER SUSAN.
MRS. DEAN'S WAY. WHAT SHE SAID and
DR. DEAN'S WAY. PEOPLE WHO HAVEN'T TIME

Each volume 16mo. Cloth. Price, $1.00.

NEXT THINGS. MRS. HARRY HARPER'S
PANSY SCRAP BOOK. AWAKENING.
FIVE FRIENDS. NEW YEAR'S TANGLES.
SOME YOUNG HEROINES.

Each volume 16mo. Cloth. Price, $.75.

GETTING AHEAD. JESSIE WELLS.
TWO BOYS. DOCIA'S JOURNAL.
SIX LITTLE GIRLS. HELEN LESTER.
PANSIES. BERNIE'S WHITE CHICKEN.
THAT BOY BOB. MARY BURTON ABROAD.
SIDE BY SIDE. Price, $.60.

The Little Pansy Series, 10 vols. Boards, $3.00. Cloth, $4.00
Mother's Boys and Girls' Library, 12 vols. Quarto Boards, $3.00
Pansy Primary Library, 30 vol. Cloth. Price, $7.50.
Half Hour Library. Octavo, 8 vols. Price, $3.20.

YENSIE WALTON. By Mrs. S. R. Graham Clark. Boston: D. Lothrop & Co. $1.50. Of the many good books which the Messrs. Lothrop have prepared for the shelves of Sunday-school libraries, "Yensie Walton" is one of the best. It is a sweet, pure story of girl life, quiet as the flow of a brook, and yet of sufficient interest to hold the attention of the most careless reader. Yensie is an orphan, who has found a home with an uncle, a farmer, some distance from the city. Her aunt, a coarse, vulgar woman, and a tyrant in the household, does her best to humiliate her by making her a domestic drudge, taking away her good clothing and exchanging it for coarse, ill-fitting garments, and scolding her from morning till night. This treatment develops a spirit of resistance; the mild and affectionate little girl becomes passionate and disobedient, and the house is the scene of continual quarrels. Fortunately, her uncle insists upon her attending school, and in the teacher, Miss Gray, she finds her first real friend. In making her acquaintance a new life begins for her. She is brought in contact with new and better influences, and profiting by them becomes in time a sunbeam in her uncle's house, and the means of softening the heart and quieting the tongue of the aunt who was once her terror and dread. Mrs. Clark has a very pleasing style, and is especially skilful in the construction of her stories.

"Yensie Walton" is a story of great power, by a new author. It aims to show that God uses a stern discipline to form the noblest characters, and that the greatest trials of life often prove the greatest blessings. The story is subordinate to this moral aim, and the earnestness of the author breaks out into occasional preaching. But the story is full of striking incident and scenes of great pathos, with occasional gleams of humor and fun by way of relief to the more tragic parts of the narrative. The characters are strongly drawn, and, in general, are thoroughly human, not gifted with impossible perfections, but having those infirmities of the flesh which make us all akin.

Little Folks' Every Day Book.

RYHMES AND ILLUSTRATIONS FOR EVERY DAY.

MAY 18TH.

A song of a nest: —
There was once a nest in a hollow;
Down in the mosses and knot-grass pressed,
Soft and warm, and full to the brim:

MAY 19TH.

"Good night!" said the hen, when her
supper was done,
To Fanny who stood in the door,
"Good night," answered she, "come back
in the morn,
And you and your chicks shall have more."

MAY 20TH.

There's a merry brown thrush sitting up
in the tree,
"He's singing to me! He's singing to
me!"
And what does he say, little girl, little boy?
"Oh, the world's running over with joy"

Edited by AMANDA B. HARRIS.

TWELVE COLOR DESIGNS EMBLEMATIC OF THE MONTHS,
By GEORGE F. BARNES.

Square 18mo, tinted edges, $1.00.

D. LOTHROP & CO., Publishers, 30 and 32 Franklin St., Boston.